Topz SECRET STories

PANTOMIME Pandemonium

Alexa Tewkesbury

CWR

Copyright © CWR 2013

Published 2013 by CWR, Waverley Abbey House, Waverley Lane, Farnham, Surrey GU9 8EP, UK. Registered Charity No. 294387. Registered Limited Company No. 1990308.

The right of Alexa Tewkesbury to be identified as the author of this work has been asserted by her in accordance with the Copyright, Designs and Patents Act 1988, sections 77 and 78.

All rights reserved. No part of this publication may be reproduced, stored in a retrieval system, or transmitted, in any form or by any means, electronic, mechanical, photocopying, recording or otherwise, without the prior permission in writing of CWR.

See back of book for list of National Distributors.

All Scripture references are from the Good News Bible, copyright © American Bible Society 1966, 1971, 1976, 1992, 1994.

Concept development, editing, design and production by CWR
Illustrations: Mike Henson at CWR
Printed in Croatia by Zrinski
ISBN: 978-1-85345-916-0

Hi there!
I'm Kevin – I'm in the Dixons Gang.

You might have heard of us. There's me and my mates, Rick and Clyde, and we all live on the Dixons Estate, in Holly Hill.

There's not that much to do in Holly Hill so we like to hang out together. The best places are the shopping centre and the park – there's lots of room there to play football or ride a bike.

Sometimes we run into the Topz Gang. 'Topzies' we call them just cos it bugs them. They're really annoying – they always seem to be talking about God and I don't get it. Us Dixons, we're cool. But Topz, they're just a waste of space.

One time we went head to head with Topz in a fundraising competition. I didn't really care who won – that's not why I wanted to enter. But then something happened to change all that.

That's what this story is all about …

Hi! We're the Topz Gang –

Topz because we all live at the 'top' of something … either in houses at the top of the hill, at the top of the flats by the park, even sleeping in a top bunk counts! We are all Christians, and we go to Holly Hill School. We love Jesus, and try to work out our faith in God in everything we do – at home, at school and with our friends. That even means trying to show God's love to the Dixons Gang who tend to be bullies, and can be a real pain!

If you'd like to know more about us, visit our website at www.cwr.org.uk/topz. You can read all about us, and how you can get to know and understand the Bible more by reading our *Topz* notes, which are great fun, and written every two months just for you!

One

'Kevin!'

Kevin's mum was yelling up the stairs to her son before she'd even put the phone down. Her face was pale and a frown pinched her eyebrows together.

Kevin appeared on the landing. He could tell from his mum's voice that something was very wrong.

'What is it?'

'It's your grandad,' his mum gulped. 'He's had another fall. Cut his head and everything. I've got to get round there now. Come with me, will you, in case I need a hand.'

Kevin didn't say a word. He just ran down the stairs and thrust his feet into the trainers he'd kicked off by the front door.

His mum hurried into the kitchen.

'Mike,' Kevin heard her say to his stepdad. 'Mike, I've got to go to Dad's. He's fallen over again. I think he might have really hurt himself this time. I'm sorry but I'm going to have to take the car.'

'What?' Mike groaned. 'But *I* need the car. I'm going to Tony's, remember? We're watching the match. Why can't you walk to your dad's?'

'I need to get there sharpish, Mike!' Kevin's mum snapped. 'And when I get there, I might need to take him to hospital! I'm sorry if it messes up your plans for watching the football, but I think my dad's just a little bit more important, don't you?'

Outside, Kevin slid into the car seat next to his mum. 'What's happened to Grandad this time?' he asked.

'Not sure,' said his mum quietly. 'Sounds like he fell over in the garden.'

Kevin's grandad had moved to Holly Hill about six years ago, when Kevin was still quite small. His nan had died a long time before. Kevin had never known her. Now Grandad lived by himself in a ground floor flat on Billings Road on the far side of the shopping centre.

Kevin was only two years old when his dad had died, and he didn't get on with his stepdad, Mike. But he was very fond of his grandad. When he was small, Kevin used to love spending time with him because Grandad was always so interested in 'little Kevin'. He wanted to listen to his grandson reading. He enjoyed hearing about the art projects Kevin might be doing at school, or the history topic the class was learning about. He liked helping Kevin with his maths, too.

'I can't do much but adding up and taking away,' he'd grin if Kevin was ever stuck on some homework, 'but let's have a look at it, eh?'

Kevin didn't go to Holly Hill School any more. He went to Southlands Primary instead, a new school on the edge of the Dixons Estate. But while he was still at Holly Hill and his mum was at work, it was Grandad who was often standing outside the school gate at the end of the day ready to meet him. They might go for a walk in the park, or back to Grandad's flat for a snack of toasted crumpets. Grandad let Kevin spread each crumpet extra thickly with butter – much more than his mum would have allowed him if he'd had crumpets at home. But she never bought them.

'Ugh! Too stodgy!' she'd say when she called to pick Kevin up. She'd wrinkle her nose as the toasting smell floated towards her from the tiny kitchen.

When Kevin was a little bigger, his after-school expeditions with Grandad got more adventurous.

'I've never really been a football man,' Grandad told him. 'Now, tennis is different! There's a game everyone should learn to play.'

One afternoon, he met Kevin after school, clutching a pair of plastic tennis rackets and a bag of tennis balls he'd just bought from the toyshop.

'Come with me,' he grinned and, before long, he was opening the gate to one of the tennis courts at the far end of the park.

'Are we really going to play tennis?' exclaimed little Kevin excitedly.

'Well,' said Grandad, 'it'll be a while before you can really "play". But I'll teach you everything I know. How's that?'

As it turned out, Grandad didn't really know very much. But he showed Kevin how to hold the racket. He told him never to take his eyes off the ball. And every now and then, they'd even manage to hit it backwards and forwards between them five or six times. Often, it was Grandad who couldn't knock it back. The ball might go sailing past him too high to reach, or fly so low that it got stopped by the net. Sometimes Grandad would blame his legs for not running fast enough. Other times he'd blame his glasses for not helping him see well enough. He never blamed little Kevin, even when his grandson knocked the ball so high into the air that no one in the whole world would have been able to hit it back.

Grandad didn't have a garden of his own. There was a small square of grass at the front of the flats. A path of pinkish-grey, square paving slabs led across it to the main entrance. Grandad always called this 'the garden'. His kitchen window looked out over it. On sunny days in summer, he'd set up a folding chair on the grass under the window, then sit there with a cup of tea and read the newspaper. He had a folding stool, too, for little Kevin, and sometimes they'd perch together side by side and watch all the different cars driving along Billings Road.

Not having a proper garden didn't stop Grandad from growing things either. Before he moved to the flat, he'd grown vegetables and flowers in the garden of his old house. When he came to Holly Hill, he began what he called 'tabletop gardening'. He pushed three long, low tables under three of the flat's sunniest windows in the lounge and the bedroom. Each tabletop held flowerpots sprouting with the herbs and red geraniums he'd planted.

'Geraniums were your nan's favourite flower,' he told little Kevin. 'The scarlet ones, of course. She loved the colour scarlet, did your nan. She'd be pleased to bits to think I was still growing them.'

Kevin's mum was always complaining, 'Dad, there's really not room for all this extra junk in here. This is only a small flat, you know. You're making it ever so difficult for yourself.' But Grandad would just look at Kevin and give him a wink. Nothing was going to part him from his flowerpots.

One day after school, Grandad had another surprise for Kevin. It wasn't tennis this time. Grandad hurried him back to the flat. There was a small, plastic tray full of soil next to the flowerpots on one of the low tables in the lounge. It all looked a bit of a squash as there were already so many pots sitting on it.

'You and me, Kevin,' Grandad said, 'are going to be gardeners today. We're going to plant some cress seeds. We're going to keep them watered, and in no time at all, the little leaves will spring up. Then we can cut some off and sprinkle them in a sandwich with a bit of cheese.'

Grandad smacked his lips at the thought. Little Kevin beamed at him and smacked his lips, too, although he didn't have any idea what cress tasted like. Then, as the small boy scattered the tiny seeds onto the soil, Grandad's old, crinkly eyes twinkled. He loved to teach Kevin new things, and Kevin loved learning them. He hadn't found out about how things grow at home. His stepdad, Mike, kept the patch of grass at the back of the house cut, but that was about all. His mum liked flowers but always said she had enough to do keeping the inside of the house tidy, without having to worry about the outside, too.

So it was with Grandad that Kevin had planted his first seeds and watched them grow. And it was with Grandad that he'd eaten his first sandwich sprinkled with his very own, home-grown cress. And that sandwich certainly was lip-smackingly good!

That's how Kevin remembered his times with Grandad for the first three years after Grandad had moved into the flat on Billings Road. They were all, in one way or another, lip-smackingly good.

Of course, back then Kevin still had his friends – Rick and Clyde in particular. The three of them all lived on the Dixons Estate and went to the same school. But more often than not, little Kevin preferred to hang out with Grandad, which Grandad was very pleased about.

'You be careful when you're playing with those boys,'

Grandad had said more than once. 'I'm sure they're good fun lads, but I wouldn't put it past either of them to cause a bit of mischief. You don't want to get dragged into anything, Kevin. Not a sensible boy like you.'

Kevin hadn't really understood what Grandad meant. Besides, outside of school he didn't spend much time with either Rick or Clyde, so it didn't seem to matter.

But, one day, something terrible happened that changed everything.

Grandad had a stroke.

Kevin didn't have a clue what a 'stroke' was when his mum first told him. At the time, she was too upset to explain it to him properly. She just said, 'It mostly happens to old people. Something goes on in the brain. Afterwards, someone who's had a stroke …' She paused and took a deep breath. '… Someone who's had a stroke might not be able to use their body the way they used to. They might not be able to walk or use their arms or hands. Or they might not be able to talk …'

Kevin still couldn't really piece together what had happened. He couldn't imagine Grandad not being able to chat to him any more over crumpets. He couldn't imagine him not being able to use his hands to do his tabletop gardening. Or not being able to use his legs to walk to meet him from school. It seemed all the harder to understand because Kevin's mum wouldn't take him with her when she went to hospital to visit Grandad.

'Grandad needs his rest. Lots of rest,' was all she'd say. 'And it'll only upset you to see him. He looks so ill.'

Grandad carried on looking very ill for a long time. But in the end he did get much better. He learnt to walk again, although his walk was more of a shuffle after his stroke, and he had to use a stick and got tired very quickly.

He learnt to talk again, too, although luckily, his speech hadn't been too badly affected. And the stroke didn't seem to have stopped his arms and hands working either. It was just his left hand that wouldn't always do what he wanted it to.

Even so, it was still four long months before Grandad was able to start living by himself in his flat again. And Kevin didn't see him in all that time.

When they did meet again, it felt odd. Awkward. Grandad was paler and thinner and Kevin was just that little bit older. Without Grandad around after school, he'd been spending much more time with Rick and Clyde. They messed about together. They weren't always very nice to other children in their class. They'd been in trouble with their teacher a few times, too.

They were a gang now.

The gang called Dixons.

Two

'Stay with us tonight, Dad,' said Kevin's mum to Grandad. 'After a fall like you've just had, I don't think you should be on your own. Come back to our house where I can take care of you.'

Grandad looked doubtful. They'd just spent four hours in hospital. Kevin's mum had explained that Grandad had fallen over in the garden of the flats where he lived. After what seemed like a very long wait, a doctor came and had a chat with them. The cut on Grandad's head was cleaned and a dressing put on. Lots of questions were asked. Did Grandad have a headache? Was he feeling dizzy? Had he been sick? Grandad said 'no' to everything and at last he was allowed to go home.

'Keep an eye on him, though,' the doctor had said to Kevin's mum.

'I don't need keeping an eye on, and I don't need taking care of,' Grandad grumbled stubbornly. 'I want to go back to the flat.'

But Kevin's mum wouldn't hear of it.

'You can have Kevin's bed,' she said. 'You don't mind, do you, Kevin? And you can sit still and have a game of chess with your grandson if you feel up to it. You've not done that in ages.'

Along with tennis and gardening, chess was something else Kevin had learnt with Grandad. Mike wasn't interested in playing games and his mum always seemed too busy. Kevin had got quite good at chess, too. He'd even won the last game they'd played together. That was quite a while ago now.

After his stroke, Grandad didn't seem so interested in the things he'd enjoyed doing before. He wasn't nearly as lively. He lost his temper more often, too. He went to sleep a lot in the daytime. And lately, he was growing more and more forgetful.

Kevin still loved his grandad, of course he did. But doing things with him just wasn't as much fun as it used to be. These days, being around him made Kevin feel sad. He couldn't help it. He didn't like to see Grandad changing. Getting older. So he'd rather be out with Dixons.

On the way home from the hospital, they called into Grandad's flat to pick up the things he'd need to stay with them for the night.

'Where do you keep the chess set, Dad?' Kevin's mum asked.

'Don't worry about it, Mum,' muttered Kevin.

'No, Kevin, let's take it. Where is it, Dad?'

Grandad couldn't remember. Kevin's mum searched through a couple of drawers. Then she looked in a cupboard. There was no sign of it.

'Honest, Mum, don't worry,' Kevin insisted. 'I'm going out when we get home anyway.'

Kevin's mum frowned. 'I don't think you are, Kevin,' she said sternly. 'I'd like you to stay at home and help look after Grandad.'

'You don't need my help,' Kevin grunted. 'You'll be all right, won't you, Grandad? You can watch TV. And I don't mind that you sleep in my bed. I can be downstairs on the sofa. I'll be back later anyway.'

When they got home, Mike was still out. Kevin's mum settled Grandad into an armchair in the lounge and Kevin carried his bag up to his bedroom. In a few moments he was back downstairs in the kitchen.

He grabbed a slice of bread and spread it thickly with peanut butter.

His mum came in to make a pot of tea. 'Don't fill up too much, Kevin,' she said. 'I'm going to get us all something to eat as soon as I've made Grandad a cup of tea.'

'I'll have mine later,' Kevin mumbled through a mouthful of bread. 'I'm going out now.'

'Kevin, no!' snapped his mum.

'But I'm supposed to meet Rick and Clyde down the park.'

'I know that,' his mum sighed. 'But, you could at least wait until we've all eaten together.'

'No.' Kevin shook his head. 'It'll be too late. They'll be going home.'

'Right.' His mum took a couple of teabags and dropped them tiredly into the teapot. 'No sign of Mike coming home either. So, it's just me and your grandad then. Same as usual these days.'

Kevin stuck his head round the lounge door on his way out. He was going to say goodbye to Grandad but, when he saw him, he changed his mind. Grandad's head was resting against the soft, comfy back of the armchair. He'd fallen fast asleep.

The Topz Gang were all sitting on a blanket on the lawn in Paul's garden. They were having a meeting.

'Anyone want another ice lolly?' Paul's mum called from the back door.

Paul glanced round at his friends, who shook their heads. 'No thanks, Mum,' he called back.

15

His mum raised her eyebrows. 'What, not even Benny?'
Benny grinned. 'No, but thanks anyway. I had one
and a half pizzas and two helpings of rhubarb crumble
and ice cream for supper! There's just no more room!'

Topz had tried to have their meeting in the park, but Rick and Clyde were hanging around there, too, and they wouldn't leave them alone. It didn't do for the Dixons Gang and the Topz Gang to be anywhere near each other. Dixons were always finding new ways to annoy them.

That afternoon, when Rick and Clyde had spotted Topz sitting in the skateboard area, they'd set their sights on being as irritating as possible. Unfortunately, the park grass had just been cut. The two Dixons boys scraped up handfuls of cuttings that the lawnmower had left behind. Then they kept running at Topz and throwing the cut grass at them. It dropped into their hair and trickled down their necks. Sarah jumped up, brushing herself off and shaking her head.

'Eeww! Get it off me!' she shrieked. 'There could be ants in it!'

Rick and Clyde fell about laughing.

Benny stood up, too. 'I don't know why you're laughing,' he muttered. 'You're not funny.'

'Maybe not,' Clyde spluttered. 'But Sarah is!'

'Let's go,' said Dave. He didn't want Benny to end up in an argument. Dixons and Topz didn't get on. They never had done. Now was the time to leave.

'But we haven't finished our meeting,' complained Josie. 'We haven't decided anything.'

Paul shrugged. 'Well, I'm starving now anyway. Why don't we all go home and then meet up after supper at my house?'

'Great idea,' said John.

Sarah was still wriggling and jiggling her head about to get rid of the unwanted grass as they walked out of the park.

Since Paul's mum couldn't persuade Topz to have another ice lolly, she brought out a tray crammed with glasses of blackcurrant squash.

Paul stretched his legs out on the blanket. 'So, what are we doing?'

Holly Hill School and Southlands, the two primary schools in Holly Hill, were running a competition. Children in years five and six from each school had the chance to get into teams to raise money for charity. There could be up to ten children in a team, and each team could decide which charity they were going to support.

Not only was this good news for the charities that were chosen, there was also a prize for the team that raised the most money – an afternoon at the quad bike centre! That was all the encouragement Topz needed.

'We've talked and talked,' Paul added, 'and so far all we seem to have decided is that we want to enter as "Team Topz".'

'Well, that's a good decision,' said Danny.

'I know,' answered Paul. 'But what are we actually going to *do*?'

John's face suddenly lit up. 'Why don't we have a car boot sale?' he suggested eagerly.

'In case you haven't noticed,' sighed Sarah, 'we don't drive. That means we haven't got cars, and if we haven't got cars, we haven't got boots.'

'We could always ask our parents,' said Josie. 'We could go round collecting lots of stuff to sell. Then they could park their cars wherever the sale's on and go home again while we do the selling.'

'But we have to do everything as Team Topz,' Sarah argued. 'There's no way Team Topz can have parents in it.

It'd be against the rules.'

'Why?' said John. 'We could be in charge. We'd only be borrowing their car boots.'

Dave shook his head. 'No, I think Sarah's right. We're supposed to do something by ourselves. And if we have to have help, then that's not really by ourselves, is it?'

The Gang fell silent again as they sipped their blackcurrant.

'Sponsored cycle ride?' suggested Benny.

Danny wrinkled his nose. 'Good idea but not very ... unusual. I mean, it'd be good fun,' he added, 'but we've done sponsored cycle rides before.'

Benny nodded slowly. 'What about a sponsored ice-skate, then? We haven't done one of those before.'

'How do you do a sponsored ice-skate?' asked Josie.

Benny thought for a moment. Then, 'Not sure,' he shrugged.

'I'd be rubbish at a sponsored ice-skate,' said Paul. 'I can never get the whole way round the rink without falling over.'

There was another silence.

'What about doing a muffin sale in the church hall?' said Dave. 'If we baked about twenty muffins each, that'd be ... well ... a lot of muffins.'

'Same as the bike ride, though, isn't it?' replied Danny. 'We've kind of done it before.'

Sarah heaved a big sigh. 'Oh, this is stupid,' she grumbled. 'How can we enter the competition if we can't even think of anything to do?'

'What we need,' said Josie, 'is for all of us to be celebrities.'

'How would that help?' John frowned.

'Well, if we were all celebrities,' Josie went on,

'then we could advertise that we were going to be hanging around somewhere on a particular day –'

'Like where?' John asked.

'I don't know. The park? The shopping centre? Anyway, it doesn't really matter where. If we were celebrities and people knew we were going to be *somewhere*, then they'd want to come and meet us. Hundreds and hundreds of people would probably turn up. Then we could sell our autographs for 50p a go. We'd make loads of money!'

Josie glanced round. The Gang were all looking at her as if she was mad.

'What?' she said. 'It's a good idea. At least it would be if we were celebrities.'

For a moment, no one said anything. Then suddenly, Sarah's mouth dropped open and she leapt to her feet.

'Josie, you're a genius!' she cried.

'I know I am,' answered Josie. 'Trouble is, I'm not a celebrity genius.'

'We don't need to be celebrities to do what celebrities do!' Sarah beamed.

Benny looked confused. 'What do you mean? What do celebrities do?'

'Exactly!' Sarah went on. 'What *do* celebrities do? Well?'

No one answered. No one had any idea what Sarah was getting at.

'Think about it!' she went on eagerly. 'When celebrities want to raise money, what do they sometimes do? They put on a show! You know, a comedy show or maybe a music concert. We've seen them on TV.'

'Yeah, but this is about Team Topz, Sarah,' said John.

'They're hardly going to put on a show for *us*, are they?'

'And anyway,' added Danny, 'you said having help was against the rules.'

Sarah looked exasperated. 'You're just not getting it, are you? We don't need celebrities. *We* could put on the show ourselves! We've done performances loads of times in church. Why not do one to raise money for charity?'

Once more, silence fell as Topz slowly took in Sarah's idea.

'Well?' she asked after a moment. 'What do you think?'

'I think …' Benny murmured, '… I think … it could be **brilliant!**'

'More than brilliant,' grinned Josie. 'More than genius, even! Can you have more than genius?'

'So,' said Dave, 'what could this show be all about?'

Sarah's brain began churning again. 'What about … what about … a *pantomime*?'

'A pantomime?' said Paul. 'You only get pantomimes around Christmas. It's not Christmas, is it? We've got to do this in the summer holidays.'

'Exactly!' Sarah clapped her hands together excitedly. 'Usually you can only go to pantomimes around Christmas. So if we put a pantomime on in the middle of summer, in the open air – EVERYONE'S going to want to buy a ticket to come and see it!'

'OK,' nodded Benny slowly. 'Maybe you're right. Maybe they will.'

'Of course they will!' Sarah beamed.

'So, that's it, is it?' said Paul. 'We're sorted.'

Dave shook his head. 'Not quite. We know *how* we're going to raise the money. Now we've got to work out who we're going to raise the money *for* …'

Three

Kevin was glad his grandad was asleep when he left the house to meet Rick and Clyde in the park. It meant he didn't have to feel guilty for going out. His mum wanted him to stay at home and help her. But if Grandad was asleep there was nothing to help *with*, was there? The two of them certainly wouldn't be playing chess.

The park was quiet when Kevin got there. He only spotted a few people in the distance, walking their dogs.

'What time do you call this?' yelled a voice. It was Rick.

Kevin jerked his head round and spotted his two Dixons friends sprawled out at the top of one of the skateboard ramps.

'Yeah! Six o'clock you said!' shouted Clyde. 'That's when the big hand's sticking straight up and the little hand's pointing to the six, Kevin – not the seven like it is now!'

He wasn't cross. Nor was Rick. They'd been happy enough killing time messing around on Clyde's skateboard. It's just that if Dixons had a chance to tease each other, they always took it.

'It wasn't my fault,' grunted Kevin, clambering up the ramp to join them. 'I just had stuff going on, that's all.'

'Oh yeah, like what?' retorted Rick.

'It doesn't matter,' Kevin muttered, shaking his head. 'Just stuff.' He didn't want to talk about Grandad. The afternoon in hospital was nothing to do with Rick and Clyde. In any case, Kevin knew they wouldn't really be interested.

Oddly, though, what Kevin *did* want to talk to his friends about had everything to do with his grandad.

Although even Kevin hadn't realised it until a couple of hours earlier.

He'd wanted to meet up with Dixons to discuss the fundraising competition that Holly Hill School and Southlands Primary were running. When their head teacher had first announced it in assembly the week before, the three boys had been unimpressed.

'Right!' scoffed Rick as they'd all filed out of the hall. 'Like I really want to spend my summer holiday raising money for charity!'

'It's not for nothing, though, is it?' said Kevin. 'At least if we raised the most we'd get to go quad-biking.'

'Yeah, but guess what else?' added Clyde. 'I'll bet you anything you like that Topz will be going in for it.'

'Of course they will,' Rick smirked. 'Bunch of little do-gooders. They'll love it!'

Kevin's eyes gleamed. 'Then let's enter.'

'What?' Clyde frowned.

'If Topz are entering,' Kevin repeated, 'let's enter, too.'

'Why would we want to do what *they're* doing?'

'Because,' grinned Kevin, 'wouldn't it be so cool to raise more money than they do – and win the competition!'

'See what you mean,' nodded Clyde after a moment. 'Sounds good.'

Kevin glanced at Rick. 'Well?'

Rick was looking doubtful.

'Come on, Rick,' said Kevin. 'Let's do it. Dixons versus Topz. What do you reckon?'

'I don't know,' he replied. 'We'd have to raise a lot of money to beat the Topz Gang. They'll have all the people in their church helping them out.'

'So? We know people, too.'

'Anyway,' muttered Rick. 'I don't know any charities.

Who are we going to raise money *for*?'

Kevin raised his eyes. 'Who cares? It's not about the charity, is it? It's about beating Topz.'

That was how Kevin had felt a few days ago. It wasn't the raising money for charity that mattered. It wasn't even about the quad-biking prize, not really. What was important was the chance to win against Topz. Besides, Dixons had a long summer holiday ahead of them. Much as they hated school, sometimes they got bored without anything much to do all day long. The competition would keep them busy.

But that was before this afternoon. Before Kevin had spent several hours sitting with his mum and Grandad in hospital.

Everything had changed for Grandad a long time ago, the moment he'd had his stroke. Everything had changed for Kevin, too. And while they'd sat there in the Accident and Emergency area, waiting for Grandad to be seen by the various doctors and nurses, Kevin had suddenly realised that the charity they raised money for *was* important after all. It was important because charities help people. If Dixons raised money for a charity that helped people who'd had a stroke, then in a roundabout sort of way, they'd be helping Grandad.

Clyde had been holding his skateboard at the top of the ramp. Suddenly he let it go. It clattered down the slope and shot forward as it rolled onto the ground. Dixons watched it go, until its short journey was halted by the foot of another ramp. Rick stretched out his legs and gave Kevin a shove with his feet.

'So what's going on?' he asked.

'The competition,' Kevin answered. 'Topz are definitely going in for it.'

'So what if they are?' Rick shrugged.

'We should do it,' said Kevin. 'I've had an idea. We could do bag-packing at the supermarket where Clyde's dad works, and car-washing in the community centre car park.'

Rick sighed and fiddled with the laces on his trainers. 'Is that it?' he demanded. 'Is that why we're here? To talk about bag-packing and car-washing?'

'It's a good idea,' insisted Kevin. 'We can have buckets at the supermarket for people to put their change in. I've seen the football team from Bruford Secondary do it when they're trying to raise money. And we could put a poster up at the community centre saying when we'll be washing cars there.'

'Yeah, but why would we want to, Kev?' asked Clyde.

Kevin frowned at him. 'You *know* why. To beat Topz.' He didn't mention collecting for a stroke charity. Clyde and Rick would only ask him what the point was and he didn't feel like trying to explain. Why should they care about his grandad? He was just hopeful that they'd be keen to try to raise more money than Topz in the competition.

They weren't.

Rick looked bored. 'It's a stupid way to beat them, though, isn't it?'

'And,' Clyde added, 'what happens if we don't get as much money as they do? We'll have done all that work for nothing. Plus they'll be able to go around thinking they're better than we are.'

'Like they don't already,' muttered Rick.

'Well, we'll just have to try really hard, won't we?' Kevin persisted. 'We can do it, I know we can. Anyway, it won't all be for nothing. Whatever happens we'll still end up with the money.'

'Yes, but so what?' argued Clyde. 'It's not like we can keep it, is it? We'll have to give it all away.'

'That's the idea of raising money for charity, Clyde,' Kevin snapped. 'You *get* the money together and you *give* it to the charity.'

Clyde scowled at him. 'I know that, Kevin, I'm not stupid. What I mean is, you said the charity bit didn't matter. You said the important thing was beating Topz.'

'And it is,' Kevin said. He got to his feet. Maybe it would be easier to tell them about Grandad. Maybe then they'd want to help. It's just that what was happening to his grandad – his falling over, his forgetfulness, his frustration – it all felt private somehow. Something Kevin didn't want to talk about with anyone.

He glanced down at the two Dixons boys stretched out at the top of the skateboard ramp. No, he thought. Whatever he said, it wouldn't make any difference. Neither of them were interested in the competition.

Suddenly, Kevin thrust his hands into the pockets of his jeans and shuffled down the ramp slope. At the bottom, he turned.

'Fine!' he grunted. 'Don't bother! I don't need your help anyway. I can raise more money by myself than either of you could both together! And when I win and get to go quad-biking, I'll be going on my own. You won't be coming with me.'

'Oh, yeah, right,' Rick smirked. 'Because you're obviously going to make so much money, aren't you, Kevin?'

'Course he is, Rick,' Clyde grinned. 'There are going to be *hundreds* of people queuing so he can pack their shopping bags for them. And *thousands* waiting for him to wash their cars!'

Kevin stared at them as they carried on giggling. Then he shook his head, turned and started stalking away.

'Oi!' Clyde yelled after him. **'Where are you going, Kev?** We're only joking. Don't be stupid! Come back!'

But, Kevin didn't go back. He didn't even look round. Dixons did a lot of messing about. But this was a joke at the wrong time and about the wrong thing. He just wasn't in the mood.

He wasn't in the mood for going home either. Kevin couldn't get the picture out of his head of Grandad fast asleep in the armchair in their lounge. He seemed comfortable enough. Peaceful even. His thin, grey hair was combed back from his face. His mouth was slightly open. His pale hands with their long, bony fingers rested on the arms of the chair.

But he looked so old. So very, very old.

The thought of him growing older and older was making Kevin sad. He didn't want to watch it happening. Grandad shouldn't even *seem* this old. He used to have so much energy. He was always making Kevin laugh. The only reason he was like this now was because of his stroke.

Kevin wandered through the shopping centre. He didn't exactly make up his mind to go to Billings Road to the flats where his grandad lived. He just sort of ended up there. Grandad wasn't at home, of course, to bring out the folding stool for Kevin to sit on under his kitchen window. But Kevin sat down there anyway, on the grass. He gazed at the cars and vans and lorries as they trundled past. He'd sat there so many times with Grandad, the two of them watching the world go by. They'd been good times. Happy times. It didn't feel the same on his own.

'It is you, Kevin, isn't it?'

Kevin looked up sharply. An elderly woman was peering down at him. He'd been so lost in thought, he hadn't noticed her walking down the path carrying a bag of shopping. He recognised her, although he hadn't seen her for quite a while. She was Mrs Rawlings, who lived in the flat above Grandad's.

'How are you, dear?' she asked kindly. 'I haven't seen you in ages.'

'Fine, thanks,' Kevin mumbled.

'And how's your poor grandad? I heard he'd taken another tumble this afternoon. Is he still in hospital?'

Kevin scrambled to his feet as he shook his head. 'No. He's at our house. He's going to stay there the night. He'll be back here tomorrow probably.'

'Poor thing,' Mrs Rawlings sighed. 'Such a nice man, too. Must be very upsetting for you.'

Kevin shrugged. 'I suppose. We're sort of getting used to it.'

Mrs Rawlings gave him an understanding smile. 'So what are you doing here? Have you come to collect something?'

Again, Kevin shook his head. He wasn't sure what to say. His grandad was probably still fast asleep in the armchair in his lounge at home. How could Kevin explain that actually he felt closer to him by sitting here? On the grass under his kitchen window.

Perhaps Mrs Rawlings understood. 'Well,' she said quietly. 'He's a lovely man, your grandad. One in a million, I've always said. You give him my love, won't you, and tell him to feel better soon. And once he's home, if he needs anything – anything at all – you tell him to pick up the phone, and I'll be right down.'

She turned back towards the front door of the flats. Then she paused.

'Your grandad loves you very much you know, Kevin,' she smiled. 'He once said to me, "Since my wife died, having my little grandson around has given me a new lease of life." I've never forgotten it. So you take care of yourself, Kevin, and be a good boy,' she added. 'Because your grandad needs you.'

Kevin wasn't sure what Mrs Rawlings meant by 'be a good boy'. Perhaps she knew about Dixons and the kind of trouble they got themselves into. Perhaps she was just asking Kevin to be especially kind while his grandad was getting over his fall.

But as he headed for home, all Kevin could think about was the money he was going to raise for a stroke charity that would help people just like Grandad. With Dixons or without them.

Four

Coming up with a way to raise money for a charity was proving far easier for Topz than deciding which charity to support.

'It's got to be the animal rescue centre, hasn't it?' said Sarah after Sunday Club.

'Why?' asked John. 'There's no reason it's *got* to be the rescue centre.'

'Of course there is,' Sarah argued. 'That's where Gruff and Saucy came from, isn't it? If it wasn't for the centre, who knows what would have become of them? And can you imagine our lives without Gruff and Saucy in them? I don't think so!'

Once Sarah made up her mind about something, it tended to stay made up. Her brother, John, certainly wasn't going to be able to change it.

'The rescue centre's great, it really is,' said Dave. 'But there are lots of other charities, too. I reckon we should think about it properly before deciding. What about the homeless centre? People without anywhere to live need rescuing, too.'

'I'm not saying they don't,' replied Sarah. 'I'm just saying that the rescue centre is really important to our family, because that's where our cat and dog came from. So it's only right that I support it.'

'It's not just you raising the money, though, is it?' said Danny. 'Don't get me wrong, I think your idea of putting on a pantomime is really cool. We should definitely do it. But all of Topz are in the competition, so all of Topz need to agree on the right charity.'

Sarah raised her eyes. 'That's what I'm saying, Danny.

The right charity is the rescue centre.'

Danny glanced at Dave. 'Yes, but I sort of agree with *you*, Dave. I think we should give the money to the homeless centre. What about anyone else?'

'I like the idea of supporting an animal charity,' said Josie. 'It doesn't have to be the rescue centre especially. There are lots of others.'

'Josie!' cried Sarah. 'What do you mean? You know how important the rescue centre is! Think how many more dogs and cats like Gruff and Saucy they could take in if they had a bit of extra money.'

'And think how many more homeless people the homeless centre could help if *they* had some more money,' muttered John.

'I wasn't talking to you!' snapped Sarah. 'Anyway, the pantomime's *my* idea, so it makes sense we should go for *my* charity.'

'Well, let's not do the pantomime then,' said John.

'WHAT?' Sarah's jaw dropped open.

'Hey, hey, hey!' called Greg. The youth leader had been stacking away the chairs and tables put out in the church hall for Sunday Club. Benny and Paul were helping.

'What's all the fuss about, Topzies?' Greg asked.

'I want to raise money for the rescue centre and John says we can't because the homeless people need it more and now he says we're not even going to do a pantomime!' Sarah blurted it all out without pausing for breath.

'I didn't say that!' grumbled John. 'That's not what I said at all!'

Greg looked confused. 'Erm … no,' he said. 'You're going to have to go through all that again just a little more slowly, because I'm afraid I haven't got a clue what you're talking about.'

Sarah went to speak again, but Josie got in first. 'You know about the fundraising competition, don't you? Well, we're going to put on a pantomime. A summer one, because no one ever does that and it's Sarah's really brilliant idea. We'll raise loads of money selling tickets for the performance.' She paused and gave her best friend a big, beaming smile. 'But the thing is, now we have to decide which charity we're going to raise money for ... and we're finding it a bit difficult.'

Greg nodded. 'What have you got in mind?'

'The rescue centre and the homeless centre.'

'Good ideas,' Greg replied. 'Very good ideas. Any other suggestions?'

The Topz Gang looked at each other. 'I don't think so,' said Dave.

'Well, then,' continued Greg, 'if you can't agree on which one of the two, I think you might need to draw your charity out of a hat.'

'Whose hat?' asked Paul.

'Anyone's hat!' laughed Greg. 'In fact, I tell you what. Let's forget the hat and do it out of a box.'

He went to a cupboard in the corner of the hall and pulled out an old, plastic ice cream tub. There were a few pencils and crayons inside, and he tipped them out onto the shelf. He then tore up a couple of sheets of paper into fourteen pieces. He gave seven of them to Sarah and Josie and told them to write 'rescue' on them. The other seven he gave to John and Dave with the instruction to write 'homeless' on them.

When all the writing was done, the pieces of paper were folded up and dropped into the plastic box. Greg gave them a good shake to mix them together.

Then, one by one, he went to each of the seven members of the Topz Gang and asked them to pick one out.

'Everyone got a piece of paper?' he said finally.
They all nodded.

'Now, before you have a look and see what you've picked, just remember this: if you can't decide on a charity between you, then this is a pretty fair way of choosing one. All right? So no more arguments. It's a great thing you're going to do, raising money for a really important charity. Whichever one it turns out to be. There's no point falling out over it. Right then. Have a look and see what you've got.'

Slowly, altogether, Topz unfolded their papers.

'No!' moaned Sarah when she saw what was written on hers: 'homeless'.

Greg raised his eyebrows. 'Sarah, no arguments, remember?'

John had 'homeless', too. So did Paul. But Benny, Danny, Josie and Dave had all drawn pieces of paper with 'rescue' written on them.

'That's four rescues and three homeless,' Greg announced. 'So it looks like your pantomime is going to raise money for the rescue centre.'

Sarah cheered and bounced excitedly up and down. Dave and Danny looked disappointed.

'But if I were you,' Greg continued, seeing the expressions on their faces, 'I'd wait and see how much money you raise. The rescue centre can always be your main charity but, if you do really well and sell loads of tickets, you might feel that you've got enough money to give some to the homeless centre as well.'

'We might, but we probably won't,' said Sarah breezily.

'But we still might,' muttered John.

It was the last day of term. At lunchtime, Topz had got together to decide which pantomime they were going to put on. There were a few suggestions but no arguments this time. Everyone was agreed on *Cinderella*.

'You make sure you put up plenty of posters so I know when it's on,' Mrs Parker, Sarah and Josie's class teacher, beamed. 'I'm not missing this panto for anything.'

After school, Sarah and Josie headed straight for the newsagents. They wanted to celebrate the end of the summer term with ice creams. They also wanted to sit and eat them on one of the benches in the park and do some more pantomime planning.

As Josie stepped outside the shop, ice cream cornet in hand, her eye fell on the cards and posters that filled one of the windows. All sorts of things were being advertised, from babysitting and dog walking, to car repairs and a second-hand guitar for sale.

'We *have* to get a poster for the pantomime up in here, Sarah!' she cried. 'It's perfect! Loads of people go in and out of this shop, so loads of people will see it!'

Sarah's face lit up. 'And if loads of people know we're putting on a pantomime, then loads of people will buy tickets, and we'll raise LOADS of money for the competition!'

Josie and Sarah were so busy looking at the shop's window that they didn't spot Dixons. But the Dixons Gang saw them straightaway as they ambled along the pavement. They heard what they were talking about, too.

'A pantomime?' sneered Rick 'Is that's what you Topzies are doing for the competition? Do you really think you're going to win with a soppy pantomime?'

The two girls twisted round.

'It doesn't matter whether we win or not,' Josie said quietly. 'We just want to raise some money for our charity.'

'And it's not soppy,' added Sarah. 'We think it's a really good idea.'

'It's a good idea if you're a soppy person,' sniggered Clyde.

'So … are you entering?' asked Josie.

Clyde shrugged. 'Nothing to do with you if we are or if we aren't.'

'You're not then,' said Sarah. 'I didn't think so.'

'What do you mean by that?' Rick growled.

'Sarah!' hissed Josie. There was a warning in her voice, but Sarah took no notice.

'I didn't think you would be, that's all,' she continued. 'I don't suppose it's really your sort of thing, is it?'

A spark of anger flashed into Rick's eyes. 'How would you know what our sort of thing is?' he snapped.

'I thought you might have liked the prize, though,' Sarah added. 'The quad-biking.'

'Oh, yeah,' Clyde said. 'Of course we'd like the quad-biking. But that's not why we'd want to win. The only reason we'd enter the stupid competition at all is to see the look on your faces when we raised more money than you.'

Rick glanced at Kevin, who so far hadn't said a word. 'Kevin's got plans, haven't you, Kev? And they'll make more money than your soppy pantomime any day.'

Kevin still didn't speak. He didn't want to talk about what he was doing to anyone in case someone else pinched his ideas. He certainly didn't want Dixons telling Topz. They might be putting on a pantomime but there was nothing to stop them bag-packing and car-washing, too.

'Let's go,' he mumbled finally.

'What? Why?' asked Rick.

'I just want to go!'

Kevin started to walk away, but before the others followed after him, he heard Clyde say to the girls, 'If anyone's going to win this competition, it's Dixons. You Topzies don't stand a chance.'

As soon as Kevin was sure Sarah and Josie wouldn't be able to hear, he turned on Clyde. 'What do you mean, *Dixons* are going to win the competition? *I'm* the one entering. On my own, remember? You didn't want to.'

'So, maybe we've changed our minds,' said Clyde. 'Maybe we really do now.'

Rick grinned. 'Maybe you really want to beat Topz now, you mean,' he said.

'And?' Clyde shrugged. 'What's wrong with that?'

Kevin eyed them both. If they were actually going to help out – make up a team – that was a good thing. With three of them joining in, they could raise three times as much money. He just wasn't sure how to tell them about the charity he wanted to give the money to.

Rick and Clyde still didn't know the charity part of the competition was important to Kevin. If they did they'd probably think he was as soppy as Topz's pantomime idea – even if he told them about Grandad. In any case, it just didn't feel right to talk about him. Grandad wasn't well, and it was *his* life. *His* problems to deal with. Kevin was sure he wouldn't want him talking about them with his friends.

Simple, then. He wouldn't tell them. He'd pretend the whole competition for him was about beating Topz, just like it was for them. He could easily say the stroke charity was one he'd found on the internet. They might as well give the money they raised to that one as to any other. That way he wouldn't need to mention his grandad at all. And the private things that were going on in Grandad's life could stay private.

'OK,' Kevin said at last. 'But we can't let on what we're doing. Not till it's all organised and we're out there doing it. We don't want anyone copying otherwise we'll end up with less money.' He paused. **'So, looks like it really is Dixons versus Topz. Game on.'**

'Yeah,' smirked Clyde. 'And we'd better make sure *we* win.'

Five

When Josie woke up on the first morning of the summer holidays, she felt excited. Then her heart sank – just a little bit. She suddenly remembered what had happened the day before with Dixons.

This summer was meant to be all about raising money for charity; doing something very important that would be great fun, too. Topz had a pantomime to put on. Josie loved rehearsing with LIFE STARTS HERE, her church drama group. All the Topz Gang were a part of it. They'd turn parables and stories from the Bible into short plays, then perform them in Sunday morning services.

The pantomime, though, would be a real challenge. Topz had never done anything like it before and they'd be completely in charge! They'd have to write a proper script, and collect costumes and props. They'd have to rehearse to get it just right, make posters to put up round Holly Hill to advertise the performance, and be responsible for selling tickets. The more tickets they were able to sell, the more money they would make for the rescue centre.

From the moment Topz had decided to enter the school fundraising competition, Josie hadn't really thought about the prize: quad-biking for the winning team. Not that an afternoon's quad-biking wouldn't be fantastic. It's just that, collecting lots of money only really seemed important so that Topz could do their best for their charity.

But Dixons had changed all that.

It was as if they'd thrown down a challenge yesterday afternoon. 'If anyone's going to win this competition, it's Dixons. You Topzies don't stand a chance.' That's what Clyde had said. And, almost as soon as the words were out of his mouth, Sarah's attitude had changed.

As she and Josie had sat in the park afterwards, eating their end of term ice creams, all Sarah seemed to want to do was to win the competition, too.

'Dixons can't say things like that,' she complained. 'Why do they think they're so much better than we are? We're going to make this pantomime the best pantomime ever. So many people are going to buy tickets for it, there won't be enough room for them all – in the whole of Holly Hill. We're going to raise hundreds of pounds. No, thousands! Millions even! We're going to make more money than any of the other teams who enter. Topz are going to win this competition, not Dixons. And when it's announced that we've won, I want to be standing right next to all three of them with a camera so that I can take a photo of their loser faces!'

'Sarah!' frowned Josie. 'Why do you care what Dixons do anyway? It doesn't matter. If they're entering the competition, then that's a good thing. It means more money will be raised and another charity will get a bit of help. Even if they win, so what? It's not *about* who wins. For us, it's about helping the rescue centre. That was *your* charity idea, remember?'

'I know it's about helping the rescue centre,' Sarah answered. 'But we can help the rescue centre *and* beat Dixons. It would be awful if we lost to them now. Really awful.'

'Why?' shrugged Josie. 'We're going to have a great time putting on this pantomime. It'll be loads of fun. Who cares about winning or losing? It's not important to me.'

Sarah put the remains of her ice-cream cornet into her mouth and licked her fingers. 'Well, Josie,' she mumbled through her mouthful, **'maybe it should be.'**

Josie got out of bed and pulled back her curtains. It was early but the sun was already beaming down through a clear, blue sky. It looked as if it was going to be a perfect summer's day. Topz were all supposed to be meeting at Sarah and John's house in the afternoon. Sarah wanted them to start working out the pantomime script as soon as possible.

Sitting back down on the bed, Josie gazed out of the window. She hoped this first day of the holidays would be a good one, but she couldn't help feeling uneasy. Sarah was going to want everything her own way. It was *her* idea. *Her* charity. And now she'd got it into her head that she wanted Topz to beat Dixons, she'd want to be in control all the more.

Josie loved her best friend. At the same time, she knew how bossy she could be. The pantomime was a good idea, it really was. But only if Topz were all working together. If Sarah was simply looking at the whole thing as a way to get the better of Dixons, Josie could see it all going horribly wrong. She wondered if her friend would have talked to God about her fundraising plans. Would she have invited Him to be a part of them? Whether she had or not, that wasn't going to stop Josie.

*I'm glad it's the holidays, God. I like being able to wake up when I want. Get up when I want. I'll probably still get up early most days, because that's when I wake up, so I may as well. But I love the feeling that I don't **have** to. Not for weeks and weeks and weeks! I could lie in bed all day if I wanted to. Although Mum would probably think I was being really lazy and make sure she set me all sorts of housey things to do so that I had to get up.*

And there's no homework either! Whoop-whoop!

This summer's going to be busy, though. I don't know if Sarah's talked to You about our Topz pantomime. I'm sure she will if she hasn't already. You see, we want to raise lots of money for the rescue centre. But we've got loads to do to get it all ready for a performance. We haven't even written it yet! Please could You help us, God? It's going to be really hard on our own. Lots and lots of fun, but still really hard. And if You're there with us, it'll all work. You'll help us to do it the best we possibly can.

*I'm a bit worried about Sarah, God. I know the pantomime's her idea, and we've ended up picking her charity to support, but it's still the Topz Gang who are doing it. All of us together. And it's not about winning the competition. That's not why we're doing it. At least, that **shouldn't** be why we're doing it. Until yesterday afternoon, it wasn't. It's just that Dixons are out to beat us. Clyde said so. I don't know why Sarah cares, God, but she really does. She wants Topz to be the ones who beat them. I don't know why it matters to her. She doesn't usually take any notice of what Dixons say. She keeps out of their way, like we all try to. I'm sure she wouldn't even care if one of the other teams won the competition. She just doesn't want it to be Dixons.*

I feel bad thinking it now, but I was really surprised when they talked about entering. I never thought Dixons would care about charities or anything like that. I suppose they might just be doing it to try to beat us. Or maybe they just want to go quad-biking. But they're still going to spend time raising money for a charity, which is brilliant, isn't it? In any case, why shouldn't Dixons want to do something kind? Just because most of the time they're not very kind at all doesn't mean they don't know how to be. So I'm sorry, God. It's as if all I expect them to be is bad.

What You want – what You ask us to do, God – is to put You first. If we put You first, that means we're talking to You and listening to You, and doing the things You want us to – not being selfish and thinking about what we want all the time. So, what I want to ask You is, please help Sarah to put You first in this competition. We all need to put You first, I know that, but I think Sarah does more than any of us right now. It can't be about beating Dixons. I don't even think it should be about winning the prize. I think we should be raising money for the rescue centre because, like Sarah says, the more money they've got, the more poor animals they can help.

Please help Sarah to see that, God. Please be there at our meeting about the pantomime today. I really want what we're doing to be a good thing – not just a way for Topz to come out on top.

Six

As Kevin unlocked the front door, he could hear the phone ringing. No one was answering. Mike and his mum were at work.

Kevin ran through the hallway into the kitchen. He half expected whoever was calling to ring off before he had a chance to pick up the phone. They didn't.

It was his mum.

'Kevin, where have you been? **I've been ringing and ringing.**'

'I've been out, haven't I?' Kevin answered moodily. 'If I had a mobile, you'd be able to get hold of me, no problem.'

His mum sighed impatiently at the other end of the phone. 'I am *not* talking about that now. You broke your phone. Save up some money and you can buy yourself a new one. Anyway listen, would you? I need you to go round to Grandad's.'

'What?' Kevin frowned. 'Why?'

'If you'll only listen, I'll tell you!' his mum snapped. 'I arranged for the hairdresser to call in today and cut his hair for him. I told him she was coming. I wrote it down and everything. Left him a note so he'd see it every time he went into the kitchen to remind him. It was for one o'clock. Anyway, I've just had a call from the hairdresser to say that she's tried and tried, but there's no answer from Grandad's flat. She had a quick peek in at the window, too, but she says she can't see any sign of anyone. I've rung lots of times, but he's not answering. I don't know where Grandad is, Kevin.' Her voice trembled slightly. She sounded as though she might cry.

'I can't get away from work. Not right now. I need you to go round to his flat for me and see if he's all right.'

Kevin was determined not to panic. 'Why wouldn't he be all right, Mum? Grandad's *always* all right. He's probably just dropped off to sleep and didn't hear there was someone at the door. You know what he's like.'

'Go round there please, Kevin, *now*,' was all his mum said.

'I'm going, Mum,' Kevin muttered. 'All I'm saying is, he'll be all right.'

'The spare keys to the flat are in the kitchen drawer. The one next to the fridge. And, Kevin – ring me when you get there.'

Kevin put down the phone, grabbed the keys, and was back outside in seconds. He had been hungry when he'd got home. Lunchtime had just about been and gone and he hadn't had a thing to eat. But as he shot out through the front door on his way to Billings Road, food was the last thing on his mind.

Kevin marched along the pavement quickly, but before long he'd broken into a run. He kept having to dodge round people in front of him who were moving too slowly. They were taking up space on the pavement, just ambling along. Why were they in his way? Where were they all going? Kevin had somewhere vital he needed to be, and fast, and everyone around him seemed to be wasting time! More than once he had to leap into the road to avoid getting stuck behind slow-moving pedestrians.

'He's all right ... Grandad's all right ...' He kept saying it to himself. Over and over again as his feet pounded along. If he said it enough times, maybe he'd even make himself believe it. He had to keep calm. If Grandad had fallen over again, or if he was ill in bed and couldn't get up, Kevin would need to be able to help him. He'd need to be able to think clearly what was the best thing to do. How could he help anyone if he was upset?

At last he saw the sign for Billings Road. Turning the corner, already breathless, Kevin forced himself into a final sprint.

At the main entrance to the flats were the names of the people who lived there, one underneath the other in a long list. There was a button beside each one which, when pressed sounded a buzzer inside whichever flat you were visiting. The person whose flat it was could then talk to their visitor through an intercom before letting them in through the main door of the building.

Kevin had the keys to the main door, and to the front door of Grandad's flat. But he thought he'd just try buzzing first. As he pressed the button and waited, what he wanted more than anything – more than *absolutely* anything – was for his grandad to answer: 'Who is it?' 'It's me, Kevin.' 'Kevin! What are you doing here? Come on in and I'll put the kettle on.'

That was what Kevin longed for. *That* was the conversation he was desperate to have. Grandad's voice would sound scratchy. It always did through the intercom. But it would mean his grandad was there. Safe. Everything would feel normal again.

Kevin stood very still, waiting. No answer came at all.

Just as the hairdresser had found earlier, there was only silence.

He fumbled in the pocket of his jeans and dragged out the keys. The longer one unlocked the main entrance door. The stubby one would let him into the flat. As Kevin slipped inside the building, his heart started to thud. Supposing Grandad wasn't all right? Supposing he hadn't answered the door to the hairdresser because he couldn't? Because he'd fallen and banged his head really hard this time? Or worse, supposing he'd had another stroke?

Kevin could feel hot tears springing into his eyes. He wanted his grandad to be fine. Fast asleep in his armchair, or having a rest in bed. If he wasn't all right, Kevin didn't want to be the one to find him. Why was his mum making him do this? *Why?* It wasn't fair. He wouldn't know what to do. If Grandad was in trouble, Kevin wouldn't have a clue where to start.

Outside the front door of the ground floor flat, the Dixons boy rubbed his eyes angrily. 'Grandad'll be fine,' he muttered to himself. 'Stop being such a baby. Grandad's always fine.' Then he took a deep breath and pushed the key into the lock. It twisted easily and in a second the door was open.

Kevin stood there, looking into the small entrance hall. He didn't step inside. Not straightaway.

'Grandad?' He spoke quietly. Anxiously. 'Grandad, are you here? Is everything all right?'

There was no answer.

Kevin waited, watching and listening for a few moments.

'Grandad?' he said again.

Inside the flat nothing moved. Finally, Kevin made himself walk in through the open door. He was scared but at the same time, he had a strong feeling that his grandad wasn't actually there. A quick peep into each room told him he was right. The flat was empty.

Kevin wasn't sure whether to feel relieved or even more worried. His mum liked to know where Grandad was all the time lately. She didn't think he was well enough to go far on his own – certainly not without letting her know first. And he was supposed to be here this afternoon because she'd arranged for his haircut. So where was he?

Perching on the edge of Grandad's armchair, Kevin picked up the phone to ring his mum. But he'd hardly begun to tap out the number when he heard a woman's voice in the corridor outside.

'Oh, my goodness! Your front door's open! You closed it behind you, I'm sure you did.'

As Kevin turned to see who was there, he recognised Mrs Rawlings, Grandad's neighbour from the flat upstairs. She looked even more anxious than he felt as she peered through the doorway. Kevin jumped to his feet.

'Kevin!' Mrs Rawlings exclaimed. 'You just gave me the fright of my life, dear! I thought your poor grandad must have had burglars!'

Before Kevin had a chance to answer, Grandad shuffled past her. He looked almost irritated, Kevin thought.

'Kevin?' he mumbled. 'What's going on? What are you doing here?'

'I came to see if you were all right, Grandad.' Kevin's face suddenly broke into a huge grin as a rush of relief swept through him. 'Mum was worried. She'd arranged for the hairdresser to call and you didn't answer the door. Or the phone. She thought maybe you weren't well again or something.'

Grandad looked confused. 'It's your mum's fault. She said something about a haircut, but she was supposed to be here to take me. I'd never have got it done at all if it hadn't been for Edie here.' He nodded towards Mrs Rawlings.

It was Kevin's turn to look confused. 'But Mum arranged for the hairdresser to come to the flat. At one o'clock. She did tell you. She said she left you a note, too. In the kitchen.'

'Nonsense,' Grandad grumbled. 'There's no note.

I'd have seen it, wouldn't I? Your mum doesn't know the time of day sometimes.'

Kevin knew that wasn't true. His mum would never have made a mistake like that. Besides, the hairdresser had been to the flat. That's how his mum had found out Grandad wasn't answering the door.

There was an awkward pause.

'Shall I put the kettle on?' asked Mrs Rawlings. 'Come and help me make a cup of tea, will you, Kevin? And you sit yourself down, Charlie,' she said to Grandad. 'Here you are, let me put the television on for you.'

Grandad settled himself into his chair and Kevin followed Mrs Rawlings into the kitchen.

Once they were inside, she pushed the door to and spoke to Kevin in a low voice so that Grandad wouldn't hear.

'I'm sorry, Kevin. I hope I didn't do the wrong thing.'

'What do you mean?' Kevin asked.

'I found your grandad at the bus stop when I went out to get the bus down to the shopping centre,' she continued. 'He wasn't looking himself at all. I asked him if he was all right and he said he was supposed to be getting a haircut, but your mum hadn't made an appointment for him and he wasn't sure where the hairdressers was. I said not to worry. He could come on the bus with me and I'd take him to mine. Such a nice girl cuts my hair,' she smiled. 'And she's made a lovely job of your grandad's, too.' But she looked concerned again when she added, 'I *am* sorry, though. I didn't realise your mum had arranged something else or I'd never have suggested it.'

'It's not your fault,' Kevin mumbled. 'I'm just glad he's all right. I need to ring Mum and tell her.'

'Well, you go and do that and I'll make a pot of tea,' Mrs Rawlings replied.

At the same time, they suddenly both spotted the note Kevin's mum had left about the mobile hairdresser visiting. It was lying on the worktop right next to the kettle.

Mrs Rawlings glanced back at Kevin. He was upset, she could see that.

'Now don't you worry yourself, dear,' she said kindly. 'It's not that long since he had his tumble outside, is it? No wonder he's still a bit confused.'

Kevin nodded, then went to phone his mum. All he said to her was that Grandad was fine and he'd explain what had happened properly later. He didn't want to tell her everything with his grandad sitting right beside him.

Hardly had he put the phone down than Mrs Rawlings was at the kitchen door.

'I think you're out of tea bags, Charlie,' she said. 'I'll pop up home and bring you some of mine.'

'You'll do no such thing,' said Grandad, but not unkindly. 'You've done quite enough for me today, Edie. I'll nip out and buy some.'

Kevin frowned. 'I don't think you should, Grandad. I think Mum wants you to stay here and have a rest. She's coming over as soon as she's finished work.'

'All the more reason to go and buy some teabags, then,' Grandad answered, heaving himself out of the chair. 'So she can have a cuppa when she gets here.'

Seven

Kevin couldn't let Grandad go back to the shopping centre on his own. His mum would worry. *He'd* worry, too. Kevin wanted to be sure he made it there and back to his flat safely. Especially as Grandad didn't want to go on the bus this time.

'I'll walk with you then, Grandad,' Kevin sighed.

'There's no need,' Grandad muttered. 'I may be a bit unsteady on my pins these days, but you don't have to fuss around me as if I'm a baby.'

'He's not fussing, are you, Kevin?' said Mrs Rawlings. 'He just wants to spend a bit of time with his grandad. When was the last time you both went for a walk together, eh? A long time, I'll bet.' And she gave Kevin a wink.

Mrs Rawlings was right. It *was* a long time ago. Kevin couldn't remember when exactly, or where they'd gone. But he knew it would have felt comfortable back then – happy, the two of them strolling along together.

It didn't feel comfortable at all that afternoon. Grandad was grumpy for a start over the muddle with his haircut. Kevin had a feeling that perhaps he knew he was the one who'd got confused. He just didn't want to admit it.

Then there was the fact that it was all the wrong way round. It was Kevin looking after his grandad instead of Grandad being the one in charge as it used to be. Kevin needed to make sure he didn't fall; he didn't get too tired. He needed to keep an eye on him all the time, because if anything happened to him while they were out, Kevin was sure it would be all his fault.

Grandad wasn't very chatty today, and his grandson wasn't sure what to talk about with him. They had to walk slowly, too, with Grandad's walking stick tapping along the pavement. He certainly couldn't be hurried. It felt to Kevin as if this trip out for teabags might take forever.

Finally, the Dixons boy decided he had to break the silence. 'I'm entering a competition,' he began hesitantly. 'It's to raise money for charity. I thought ...' He paused. He didn't want to mention Grandad's stroke, but at the same time he wanted his grandad to know what he was fundraising for. 'Well, I thought, because of your stroke and everything ... I'd try and get some money together to give to a stroke charity.'

Grandad didn't answer. As Kevin looked at him, he wasn't even sure he'd heard him.

'So I went to the supermarket this morning and the man I spoke to about it said I can do some bag-packing. You know, pack up people's shopping for them at the checkout. Then they can make a donation if they want to. He says I can have a bucket with a sign on saying what I'm collecting for. I'm going to do it on a Thursday afternoon in a couple of weeks.'

Grandad still didn't respond. Kevin carried on talking anyway. 'I've got to go to the community centre, too. I want to see if they'll let me do a car-washing day in the car park. Lots of people would come down to have their car washed, wouldn't they? Especially if they knew it was for charity?'

Grandad stopped walking and gave a tired sigh.

'What's wrong?' Kevin frowned. 'What's the matter? Aren't you feeling well?'

His grandad tutted. 'Will you stop worrying?

I'm feeling fine. It's just my legs. They don't want to keep up with yours.' Then a smile lifted his thin, pale mouth.

Kevin smiled back, relieved. 'Sorry,' he said. 'I'll walk slower.'

The part of the fundraising that Kevin had left out was that his two friends in the Dixons Gang would be helping him. They'd gone with him to the supermarket. Clyde's dad worked there and he'd introduced the three boys to the manager.

But Grandad didn't like Dixons. He didn't want his grandson to be part of a gang. Certainly not with boys like Rick and Clyde. It made him uneasy. He'd always known those two would be troublemakers, right from when they were little. It upset him to think that they were now Kevin's best friends.

Kevin knew it, too. So he didn't mention them.

At last, they arrived at the shopping centre. Fortunately, coming from Billings Road, the mini-supermarket was on the corner by the entrance on that side. Kevin was glad they didn't have to wander down through the other shops to reach it. All he really wanted was for Grandad to buy his teabags so that he could see him safely back home again.

As they were about to go into the shop, two things happened. First, the automatic doors opened and Sarah and Josie came out with a shopping bag.

Next, Rick and Clyde appeared in the doorway of the games shop opposite.

Bumping into Sarah and Josie wasn't a problem for Kevin. He didn't even have to speak to them unless they spoke to him first, which they probably wouldn't. But seeing Rick and Clyde was the last thing he was expecting – or wanting. Not while he was with Grandad.

Kevin turned his back towards them, hoping they hadn't spotted him.

They had. They'd seen Sarah and Josie, too.

'All right, Kev?' yelled Rick.

It was pointless Kevin pretending he hadn't heard him. Rick had shouted so loudly that even the people in the *park* must have heard him.

'All right?' he said. Then, 'I can't stop. I'm with my grandad,' he added quickly.

Grandad glanced at the two boys who'd come over to join them. He hadn't seen them in quite a while but he knew well enough who they were.

Rick and Clyde ignored him. They were far too interested in the two Topz girls who were trying to slip away unnoticed with their shopping.

'Surprised to see you two here,' called Rick. He was still talking much too loudly. 'Thought you'd be way too busy practising your panto. Or have you given up on that soppy idea?'

'We're going to rehearse now, as a matter of fact,' Josie mumbled.

'Well, not rehearse exactly,' added Sarah. 'We've got to do lots of planning first. We just needed to buy notebooks.' She indicated the shopping bag.

Kevin shifted from one foot to the other uncomfortably. 'Anyway, I've got to get on,' he said.

Clyde took no notice. 'Well, do you know what, Sarah? You're a bit behind. We've done our planning *and* our organising. We even know exactly *when* we're raising our money.'

'Really?' Sarah replied. 'And what charity are you supporting?'

Clyde knew they were going to be helping a stroke charity. Kevin had decided on a place called Hatherington House. It was a centre just outside Holly Hill that helped people who'd had strokes to get back to living a normal life again. He'd told Dixons about it because the supermarket needed to know which charity they were raising money for. Kevin hadn't mentioned his grandad, though. That part of it was nothing to do with anybody.

'You can't enter the competition unless you're fundraising for a proper charity,' Sarah added. 'So what is it?' She didn't sound as if she believed Dixons had got one.

'Like that's any of your business!' Clyde snarled.

'Come on, Sarah,' said Josie. 'We need to get to our meeting.'

'Oh, we need to get to our meeting, do we?' replied

Rick in a high-pitched voice, imitating her.

Grandad suddenly interrupted. 'What's this about then?' he asked. 'Are you *all* raising money for charity?'

Kevin looked at him. He was surprised that Grandad had been listening – even more surprised that he seemed to know what they were all talking about.

'Erm ... yes,' smiled Sarah. 'It's a competition.'

'Yes, I know all about it,' answered Grandad. 'My grandson here's been telling me. He's entering as well, you know.'

Kevin could hardly believe it. Grandad hadn't replied at the time, but he'd obviously taken in every word his grandson had said as they'd walked to the shopping centre together. One half of him was delighted. Maybe that meant his grandad was fine after all. Perhaps Mrs Rawlings was right and he was still just feeling a bit funny after his latest fall. He'd get better, though. Back to his old self.

But inside him, the other half of Kevin groaned. Now Grandad would find out that he wasn't fundraising on his own. He was doing it with Dixons. Entering the competition was a good thing, but his grandad wouldn't see it that way once he knew Rick and Clyde were involved.

'Well, Kevin's entering with us, isn't he?' Clyde said.

Grandad peered at him for a moment, then slowly he nodded his head. 'Oh. Is he?'

'Course he is!' grinned Rick. 'And we're going to raise a pile more money than anyone else,' he added pointedly, fixing his eyes on Sarah.

'You don't know that,' Sarah muttered.

Josie had heard enough. It was time to leave.

'Anyway,' she said, smiling at Kevin's grandad,

'we have to go now. It was very nice to meet you. Come on, Sarah.'

With that, she grabbed Sarah's elbow and pulled her away from the huddle of Dixons.

'Bye, then!' shouted Clyde. **'Have a soppy time in pantoland!'**

Sarah would have shouted something in response, but Josie hissed at her to be quiet and keep walking.

Kevin took the chance to get away, too. 'Come on, Grandad,' he muttered. 'Let's go and get your shopping.'

'What are you doing after that?' Rick asked.

'I'm going home with Grandad, aren't I?' replied Kevin.

'So you don't want to go to the community centre, then? Sort out the car-washing?'

Kevin shook his head. 'I can't. Not today.'

'Are we going to buy these teabags or not?' Grandad sighed.

'Look, I've got to go,' Kevin said.

'Right,' nodded Clyde. 'Well, we'll meet you at the park later.'

Kevin glanced at his grandad. 'I don't know,' he said. 'I'll have to see.'

He took a couple of steps forward and the automatic doors to the mini-supermarket swung open with a humming sound.

Grandad ambled after him. He didn't look at Kevin as he walked slowly past him in search of teabags. But as he made his way down the first aisle shaking his head, Kevin heard him mutter, 'I've said it before many times. They're mischief-makers those two lads. Makers of mischief. And leopards, as they say, *never* change their spots.'

Eight

'Sarah should *so* be Cinderella,' said Benny.

Topz's pantomime meeting had just got started. The Gang were once again sprawled on a blanket in Paul's garden. First things first: who was going to play which part?

'It makes sense, doesn't it?' Benny continued. 'If Sarah plays Cinderella, then John can be one of the ugly sisters. Not that I'm saying you're ugly, John,' he added quickly. 'But you and Sarah are twins. You look sort of like each other. So you could definitely play sisters.'

'Yes, but the ugly sisters aren't Cinderella's *real* sisters, are they?' Josie pointed out. 'They're stepsisters. So they wouldn't look alike anyway.'

'Oh, yeah.' Benny thought for a moment. 'Well, I still think Sarah would be ace as Cinderella.'

'And I wouldn't mind being an ugly sister, either,' said John.

'So how about,' began Benny again, 'Sarah's Cinderella, John's an ugly sister, I'm the other ugly sister – and Paul's the wicked stepmother? John and me, well, we're sort of the same height, and Paul's a bit shorter. That would look quite funny, wouldn't it? Two tall ugly sisters and one short wicked stepmother.'

Paul frowned. 'I'm not *that* short.'

'No, I didn't mean that,' laughed Benny. 'But you're a bit shorter than us. And maybe John and I could wear high heels or something, too. To make us even taller. What does everyone think?'

'Sounds *really* good,' replied Sarah. 'Only maybe we shouldn't call the two stepsisters "ugly". I know they're supposed to be, but it seems a bit mean to call anyone "ugly". Could they just be "the stepsisters who aren't as beautiful as Cinderella" instead?'

'Don't see why not,' Benny shrugged.

'OK,' Sarah beamed. 'As long as it's all right with you, Josie – if I'm Cinderella?'

'It's cool,' Josie smiled. 'It means I get to be your fairy godmother.'

Sarah started to scribble the list of characters and who was playing them in one of the notebooks she and Josie had bought earlier. 'So,' she went on when she'd finished writing, 'that just leaves the prince.'

'There'll have to be someone else, too,' said Josie. 'Danny and Dave both need parts.'

'Well,' answered Sarah thoughtfully, 'I was wondering ... I mean, say if it's a bad idea, Dave, because if it is then we'll make up another character ... but I was wondering if maybe Danny could be the prince, and you, Dave, could *not* be an actor but be our director instead.'

Everyone looked at Dave.

'I think Sarah's right,' agreed John. 'We probably do need a director. Someone to be in charge of rehearsals and help us to put the whole panto together. You'd be good at that, Dave, because you're really organised.'

'That's what I thought,' said Sarah. 'And when we have LIFE STARTS HERE rehearsals, you sometimes say you're not that fussed about having a part to play if there aren't enough. And you always have loads of good ideas when we're trying to work out a short scene for church. So I'm sure you'll have *tons* of brilliant ideas for the panto. What do you think?'

Dave nodded slowly. Then his face broke into a smile.

'Director Dave!' he said. 'I like the sound of that.'

'Are you sure?' asked Sarah.

'Absolutely positively positive,' Dave grinned.

'And you're cool being the prince, Danny?'

'Yeah ...' But Danny didn't look completely cool. 'I mean,' he added, 'you and me, Sarah ... Well, we won't have to, like, *kiss* or anything, will we?'

'Eeeew!' shrieked Sarah. The rest of the Gang howled with laughter. 'No chance!'

Danny's cheeks glowed a little pink as he nodded, 'Uh-huh. Just checking. I'll be the prince, then.'

'Next,' announced Sarah. 'What are we going to do about costumes? We can't really hire fancy dress because that'll take money away from the rescue centre.'

'We could ask our mums, I suppose,' suggested Josie. 'They might be able to make us something.'

Sarah shook her head. 'I don't think we'd be allowed. The rules say we're supposed to do it all ourselves, remember?'

'Then, why don't we wear our own clothes?' said Danny. 'I've got a brand-new denim jacket. I haven't even worn it yet. If I wear it with black jeans it'll look awesome.'

'And you could make yourself a crown,' said Paul. 'So everyone knows you're the prince.'

'I could wear leggings and an old t-shirt with one of mum's aprons over the top for Cinderella, before she gets to wear her party gear,' Sarah cried excitedly. 'Then I've got lots of pretty dresses I could wear for the ball.'

'I could wear a party dress, too,' added Josie. 'And I'll make myself some fairy wings. I'm sure I can, it can't be difficult.'

Benny grinned at John and Paul. 'Then the three of us can raid our mums' wardrobes!'

'We ought to have wigs, too,' replied Paul. 'My mum doesn't have a wig.'

'No problem,' said Danny. 'You can get funny wigs at the toyshop. Really cheap, too. My dad went to a fancy dress party dressed as a rock star once. He got a really long, bright red one.'

Dave raised his eyebrows. 'Bet that looked weird.'

'It did, yeah,' Danny agreed. 'Especially as Dad's got loads of hair anyway. He couldn't get it all inside the wig so quite a lot of it ended up sticking out. He didn't wear it in the end. Mum said if he did, she wouldn't go with him!'

Benny chuckled. 'Has he still got the wig, though?'

'I don't know. Probably. Unless Mum's got rid of it. Dad never throws anything away.'

'Then could you see if we could borrow it?' Benny asked. 'Long red hair would be great for one of the ugly sisters ... I mean, one of the "sisters who aren't as beautiful as Cinderella".'

Sarah made some more notes. Then, 'Right,' she said.

'Let's all sort out our costumes by the end of next week so that we can tell Dave exactly what we're wearing.'

'I think we should all meet up in our costumes, too,' added Josie. 'Just to make sure everything looks OK.'

'Good idea,' replied Sarah.

Topz agreed a day to bring all the clothes, including wigs, wings and crown, round to Sarah and John's house. Sarah then wanted to start making a list of props and small bits and pieces of furniture they might need. But Dave, as the director, decided it would be better to start working out the pantomime script. Once they knew how they were going to tell the Cinderella story, they'd have a much better idea of what props they'd need in each scene.

John looked impressed. 'You see, what did I tell you? Dave is just *so* organised.'

A 'script' meeting was arranged for the next day.

Everyone was about to leave when Sarah, stuffing her notebook into her rucksack, said, 'I suppose you've all heard that Dixons are entering the competition now?'

Benny frowned. 'What? How do you know that?'

'They were boasting about it,' Sarah said. 'How they're going to make loads more money than we are and how they don't care about raising the money for charity. All they care about is beating us.'

'Well, I'd like to see Dixons put on a pantomime,' muttered Danny. 'Whatever they're doing, they'll never even raise a millionth of what we can.'

'A zillionth even,' scoffed Paul.

'Of course they won't,' said Benny. 'And if they don't care about raising the money for charity then they shouldn't even be doing it. They definitely don't deserve to win the competition.'

Sarah pressed her lips together. 'So,' she said firmly, 'we're all agreed then. We've got to make a really, *really* amazing job of our pantomime because there's no way on earth we can let Dixons beat us.'

The Topz Gang glanced at each other and nodded. All except Dave and Josie.

'But hang on a minute,' said Dave. 'I know there's a prize but the competition's not supposed to be about winning and losing. You win a prize if you happen to raise more money than anyone else, but the most important thing is the charity. We're out to help, not win a competition.'

'Exactly!' said Josie. 'And even if Dixons *are* only doing it to beat us, at least the charity they choose will get some money.'

Sarah scowled. 'We don't know that they're even supporting a charity. We saw them earlier and they wouldn't tell us what it was, would they?'

'And why should they?' Josie answered. 'Like Clyde said, it's got nothing to do with us.'

'It has if they're going to keep the money for themselves,' Sarah snapped. 'It's not fair on the teams who are working really hard to do something good, *and* it's actually stealing, Josie.'

Josie gazed at her friend for a short moment. 'I know it's Dixons and I know what they're like,' she said quietly. 'And I know they've said that they don't care about anything as long as they beat us. But we shouldn't think that they're going to keep the money. We always do that – we *always* think the worst of them. And that can't be right. God doesn't want us to do that, does He? He wants us to look for the best in people. That's what Jesus did. And then, when Jesus *found* the best in people, they started to *be* better people.'

The Gang were all looking at her.

Josie glanced round at them. 'Well, it's true, isn't it?'

No one spoke. Then, 'Of course it's true,' Dave said. 'Dixons are trouble, we all know that. But you're right, Josie. We've got to try and stop expecting the worst of them. It's not important why they've decided to do some fundraising. The point is that they're doing it, and I'm sure they're not going to keep the money. They won't be able to anyway, not if they're entering the competition properly. They'll have had to register their charity with their school just like we did. And who knows? They might actually enjoy doing something good. Something that'll help people.'

'Or animals,' added Josie.

Sarah chewed on her lower lip moodily. 'OK,' she muttered. **'That still doesn't mean we have to let them beat us.'**

chewed her lip

Most days, Josie loved being in the Topz Gang. Most days, she loved being best friends with Sarah. Today, however, wasn't one of them. She was hurt and upset. The pantomime meeting had ended badly and all because Sarah had mentioned Dixons.

Why, God? Why did Sarah have to bring Dixons up? She's spoilt the whole day.

I wish we hadn't entered this stupid competition. It's making Sarah so mean. So ... competitive. I mean,

*I know you have to **be** competitive if you want to win a competition, but that's not what this one's supposed to be about. It's got nothing to do with Topz or Dixons. It shouldn't be about winning or losing. It's the charities that are important and what they're going to be able to do with the extra money we can give them.*

*But what I really don't understand, God, is what's happened to Sarah. This is **so** not like her. She's normally the one who wants to give Dixons a second chance. She wants to be able to talk to them about You. She'd do anything for them to know what they're missing out on by not being friends with You. And she talks to You about them loads. Much more than I do. They can be so nasty to us, but she still cares about them.*

*At least she **did**.*

*That's why I hate this competition, God, because now all Sarah seems to care about is winning. All she wants to do is to beat Dixons. I'm sure it's because the pantomime's her idea. If we were doing anything else – a garage sale maybe, or something that's more 'normal' for fundraising – I don't think she'd care at all. It's like she's trying to prove herself with the pantomime. Even after everything I said about trying to find the best in people like Jesus does, she still wants to win. She still wants to be able to prove that Topz are better than Dixons; that **she's** better than Dixons. And, can You believe it, God, because I really can't, but most of Topz seem to feel the way she does! That we've got to beat Dixons no matter what! It was only Dave who could really see what I was trying to say.*

We have to put You first, God. We have to raise this money as if we're working for You. Jesus says it in the Bible, doesn't He? Greg got us to learn the verse at Sunday Club because it's so important: '… be concerned above everything else with the Kingdom of God and with what he requires of you …' Matthew 6 verse 33. That's when You can **really** *bless us,* **really** *help something good to come out of what we're doing. Trying to get one up on Dixons isn't being concerned with You. And thinking the worst of them all the time* **definitely** *isn't being concerned with You.*

Please, God, please change how Sarah's thinking. Please help all of us – all of Topz – to look at Dixons in a different way. We need to see them through Your eyes, God.

I **want** *us to see them through Your eyes.*

Nine

'I think we might have to look into Grandad going into a care home.'

Kevin stared at his mum as she sat in the kitchen. He could hardly believe she'd said it. But as he looked into her eyes, he knew she was deadly serious.

'We can't,' he growled. 'He'd hate it. You know he'd hate it.'

His mum shook her head. 'And do you know what *I* hate, Kevin?' she asked. 'I hate the fact that Grandad keeps falling over. I hate it that he's getting confused and forgetful. I hate it that he seems to walk just a little bit slower every day. I hate it that he's got old. And what I hate more than anything,' she cried, her voice rising higher, 'is that I have to go out to work full-time and I can't be around every day to look after him!'

'*I* help, don't I?' argued Kevin. 'And I can go and visit him more.'

'Oh, Kevin. Of course you help sometimes. You go round and see him when I ask you to. You're sensible with him. It's just …' His mum sighed heavily. 'I can't have Grandad to stay with us here as often as I want to because Mike doesn't like it. He says we haven't got the space. And he's right, really. We haven't. Trouble is, it's not possible for me to keep going round there all the time either. I just think it's getting to the stage where he can't be left on his own as much as he is.'

Kevin was beginning to feel desperate. He could see his mum had already made up her mind. She was going to start looking for a care home for Grandad and nothing he said would make any difference. It didn't stop him trying, though.

'But what about his flat?' he mumbled. 'He's got it just the way he wants it. All his pots for growing things. You know how much he likes his table-top gardening.'

'Kevin, he hasn't done that for ages. You know he hasn't. He's not been well enough.'

'What about his geraniums, then?' Kevin persisted. 'He's still got some of those. The ones Nan used to like.'

'That's because I buy the odd one for him, Kevin,' said his mum quietly. 'And I can't believe that he won't be allowed a geranium on his windowsill in a care home.'

One windowsill? Is that all Grandad would be allowed? Space for one geranium on one windowsill? It sounded horrible. Kevin didn't visit his grandad nearly as often as he used to. But the thought of not being able to go and see him at his flat, where they'd shared so many happy times – the thought of him being crammed into one tiny room with one measly windowsill – was practically unbearable!

'No!' Kevin shook his head determinedly. 'Grandad won't want to go. And he doesn't have to go. He loves that flat. Even when he falls over, he's OK. He's always OK, you know he is.'

Kevin's mum got to her feet. She looked at her son tiredly. 'Grandad's been very lucky so far,' she said. 'Each time he's fallen over, he hasn't hurt himself too badly and there's always been someone around to help him back up; to give me a ring and let me know.' She shrugged her shoulders. 'But what happens, Kevin,' she continued slowly, 'when he falls down and there's no one there to help? What happens if he hurts himself and no one knows?'

Kevin gazed at his mum miserably. He could see it was hopeless.

'Grandad needs to be where someone can keep an eye on him,' his mum sighed. 'He needs to be in a care home.'

As Kevin ran out of the house, he slammed the front door hard behind him. Mike, his stepdad, had just got home from work and was getting out of the car.

'Hey!' he shouted as Kevin raced past him. 'You could have left the door open for me! Where do you think you're going in such a hurry?'

Kevin ignored him. He didn't have much to say to Mike at the best of times. At that moment, he was the last person in the world Kevin wanted to talk to. As far as he could tell, Mike didn't even like his grandad.

As Kevin hurried out of the Dixons Estate there was only one place he really wanted to be: in Grandad's flat. With Grandad. But not as things were now. The way they used to be when he was a little boy at Holly Hill Primary School. He wanted Grandad to invite him in to look at the different seeds he was growing. He wanted him to go to the breadbin and produce a packet of crumpets. 'Now then,' he wanted Grandad to say. 'Just time to toast a couple of these before your mum gets here, eh?'

Kevin's feet slowed on the pavement. Without really thinking about it, he'd been heading for Billings Road. Suddenly it occurred to him – what was the point? Grandad was most likely fast asleep. If Kevin woke him by ringing on the buzzer, it would startle him. Once, recently, he had gone to the flat with his mum and for a moment Grandad hadn't been quite sure who they were.

In any case, his mum would be dropping round there before long. She went over every evening now. Usually she took Grandad some supper so that she knew he was getting a proper cooked meal every day. Kevin didn't want to be there at the same time. He'd look at his mum, knowing she was planning to move Grandad out of his home. Then he'd look at Grandad, who knew absolutely nothing about it.

Stuffing his hands into his jeans pockets, Kevin changed direction. This time he made for the park. He had a few coins in change, so he stopped off at the newsagents and bought himself a can of lemonade. Then he crossed the road and ambled through the park gates.

It was early evening, sunny and warm. The play areas were still quite busy so Kevin walked beyond them to the trees at the edge of the football field. There, he slumped onto the ground with his back against a tree trunk. He opened the can of lemonade. It made a satisfying fizzing sound. Then he lifted it to his lips to take a long, refreshing mouthful.

That's when he almost choked.

'I'm so sorry! I didn't mean to make you jump. Are you all right?'

It was Josie. She was clutching a notebook and looked almost terrified that she'd startled the Dixons boy.

'Do I *look* all right?' Kevin spluttered. He'd been so shocked by Josie's sudden appearance that he'd dropped the can of lemonade. It was spilling onto the grass.

Quick as a flash, Josie leapt forward and grabbed it. She held it out to him.

'I don't think you've lost much,' she mumbled.

Kevin snatched it from her and stood up. He was still coughing.

'What are you doing here anyway?' he managed to say at last. 'I came here to be on my own.'

'Did you?' Josie answered apologetically. 'So did I. Sorry.'

Kevin swallowed hard a couple of times before taking another swig of lemonade. Then he sniffed and wiped the back of his hand across his mouth. His choking seemed to have stopped.

'No getting away from you Topz sometimes, is there?' he grunted.

'Apparently not,' Josie replied. 'Anyway, I didn't mean to disturb you. I was just going to sit here and ...'

Her voice trailed off. She'd planned to sit under the trees at the edge of the football field and try learning her lines for *Cinderella*. She had them all written out in the notebook she'd brought with her. But as she started speaking, she realised that mentioning the pantomime was probably a bad idea. Kevin would more than likely sneer at her and tell her that Topz didn't stand a chance in the fundraising competition. Dixons were bound to win, so why didn't they just give up now and save themselves some bother.

'What?' Kevin frowned.

'Sorry?'

'You were just going to sit here and what?'

What else could Josie say? 'I was just going to go through my lines for our pantomime, that's all,' she sighed.

Kevin nodded. Suddenly he sat back down. 'Right.'

Josie couldn't quite believe it. Was that it? Was that all Kevin had to say? No nasty comment? No spiteful laughter?

'What pantomime are you doing?' he added.

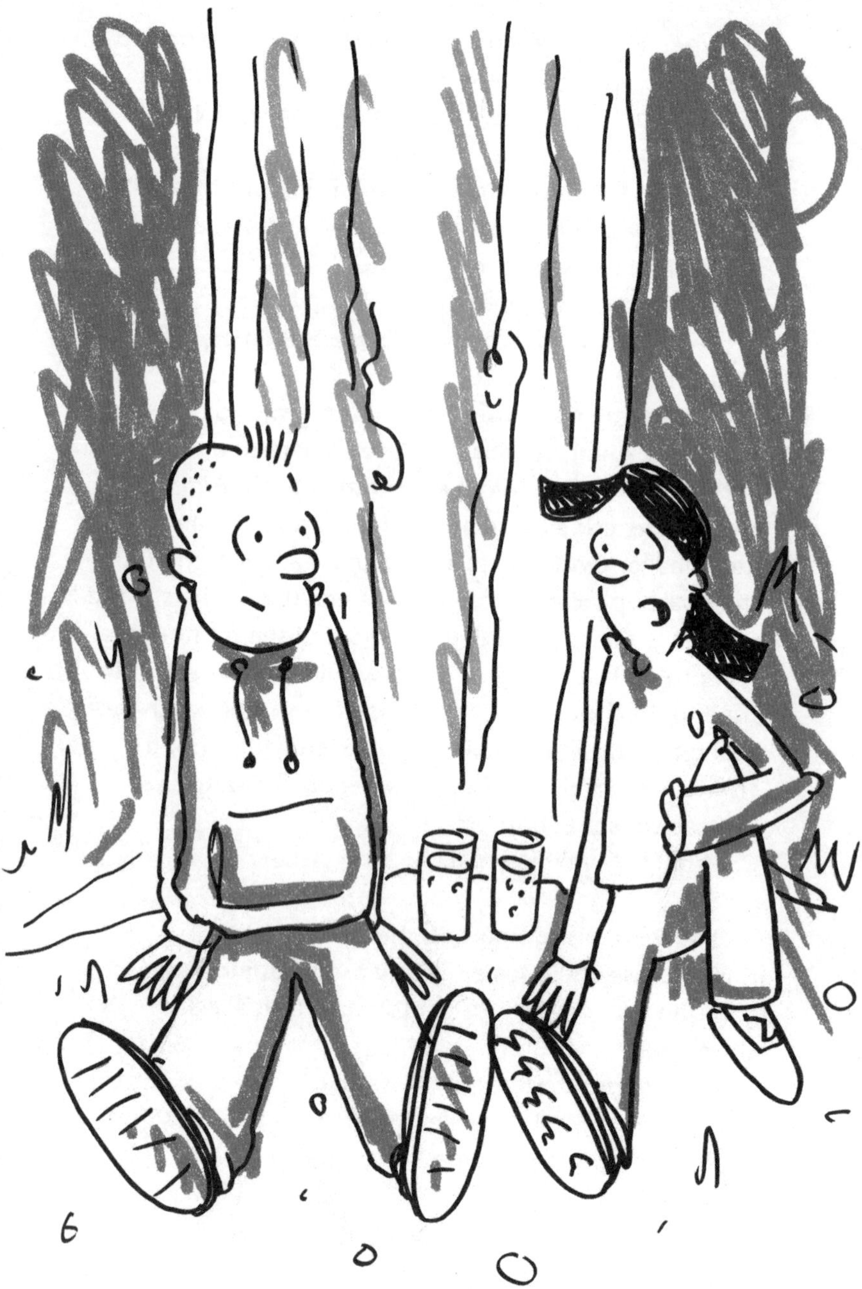

'Erm ... *Cinderella*.'

'Is that you?' he asked. 'Are you going to be Cinders?'

Josie shook her head. 'No,' she murmured. 'No, I'm the ... fairy godmother.'

Even as she said it, she felt ridiculous. You didn't talk about fairy godmothers when you were around Dixons boys.

But then Kevin took her by surprise yet again.

'Well, I think it's a good idea,' he said, sipping more of his lemonade. 'I reckon you could raise a lot of money doing something like that.'

For one awkward moment, Josie thought she was going to laugh. This whole situation was becoming more and more unreal. But as she gazed at Kevin uncomfortably, trying to work out what was going on in his head, she realised that he wasn't teasing her or trying to be funny. He actually looked very upset.

She hesitated. Should she ask him if he was all right? After all, the worst he'd probably do was tell her to get lost, and Topz were used to that from Dixons.

'Is anything wrong, Kevin?' she gulped.

His eyes flicked up at her. Almost instantly, he looked away again. He didn't answer Josie's question. Instead he asked, 'What charity are you supporting?'

'The rescue centre,' Josie answered. 'You know, the animal one in Holly Hill.' Then, 'What about Dixons?' she added. 'Have you thought of a charity yet?'

Josie thought Kevin nodded, but his head hardly moved so she wasn't completely sure.

'We chose the rescue centre because that's where Sarah and John's cat and dog came from,' Josie went on. 'Sarah wants the centre to be able to do more rescuing.'

Again Kevin nodded, very slightly. As he didn't say anything more, Josie thought that perhaps the conversation was over. She waited a moment, then took a few steps further away and went to sit down. She knew she probably wouldn't be able to learn a word of her script with Kevin sitting there, but to leave now would look odd.

'I chose our charity,' Kevin said suddenly.

Josie looked back at him.

'It's erm … Hatherington House. A centre that helps people who've had strokes.'

'Sounds brilliant,' said Josie. She could feel herself beginning to smile.

And when Kevin told her that the reason he wanted to raise money for Hatherington was because his grandad had suffered a stroke, Josie's smile spread even more.

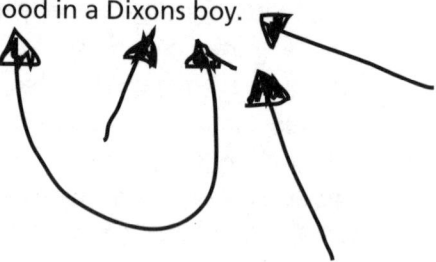

She'd just found the good in a Dixons boy.

Ten

Topz had spent ages working out the script for their pantomime. Dave and Sarah both thought the best way to do it was to start by planning what would happen in each scene. Then they could all try improvising the scenes and writing down the ideas they came up with.

To help themselves, the Gang had read as many different versions of the *Cinderella* story as they could find. Once they had their own Topz-style script worked out and scribbled down in various notebooks, they were ready to start rehearsals.

They could also set the date for the performance and the place where it was to be held. Sarah was hoping they could have put the pantomime on in the park, and was very disappointed when she found they weren't allowed to. So, instead, she'd gone with Dave and Josie to see Mr Smithson, the Holly Hill School caretaker. He only lived just round the corner from Dave's house and was good friends with Dave's dad.

To Sarah's delight, Mr Smithson said that, as far as he was concerned, they were more than welcome to use the school playing field as their pantomime venue. He said he'd have to check with the head teacher, of course, but he was sure it wouldn't be a problem. Especially as this was Topz's entry for the fundraising competition.

'Have you thought about how you're going to advertise your show?' he asked. 'How about getting people to bring a picnic along? They do that with some of those open-air concerts, don't they? You could do your own "picnic and a panto in the park" type thing. Except, of course, you won't be in the park.'

Sarah's eyes shone. 'That's such a cool idea!' she cried excitedly. 'We can put it on the posters! You know, encourage people to bring their own food and a blanket to sit on. This is going to be just the best event ever in Holly Hill!'

With the date, time and place now set for *Cinderella*, Topz still had lots to do – and just two weeks to get their performance ready.

'Do you think it's enough time?' Sarah worried.

'It's loads of time,' said Dave. 'We can rehearse every day if you want.'

Surprisingly, Josie thought, Dixons hadn't been mentioned since Sarah had first announced to Topz that the other gang were entering the competition. Josie certainly didn't want to be the one to bring them up again. She now knew which charity they were supporting because, for whatever reason, Kevin had decided to tell her. But she hadn't spoken to the rest of Topz about it. Kevin didn't mind people knowing that Dixons were helping a stroke charity. In fact they had to know what they were giving money to. What he didn't want spread around was his reason for choosing Hatherington House. So Josie had decided to keep quiet about the whole conversation. She was pleased that Topz were all so busy getting ready for their show. It meant there was less time for them to spend thinking about winning the competition.

Topz weren't the only ones who were busy. Dixons had been to the community centre to arrange to do car-washing in the car park. They were allowed one Saturday – which turned out to be the same Saturday as Topz's pantomime. The most important thing they needed to do now was to advertise the event around Holly Hill.

They wrote out twenty posters giving the time, date and place, and the name of the charity the car-washing day was raising money for. Kevin decided they should charge £2 for cars and £3 for vans. That was a lot less than it cost to use a car wash at a garage, and he hoped it would mean lots more people would turn up.

Then they tramped around Holly Hill, putting the posters up wherever they could: in the front windows of their houses; on lampposts – although Kevin knew they probably wouldn't last long if it rained; in the window of the launderette, and the windows and glass doors of whichever shops were happy for them to advertise the event there. Some of the shopkeepers raised their eyebrows. They knew Dixons as troublemakers, not fundraisers. But Hatherington was a local charity and if the community centre was helping the boys with the use of their car park, there was no reason not to let them put up a poster.

Sarah's jaw dropped when she saw the one in the newsagent's window.

'How *could* they?' she cried. 'That's where we were going to put one of *our* posters!'

'There's still room for us,' said John, pointing to a space on the glass a little higher up. 'We just need to hurry up and make them so we can start sticking them around.'

'But *look!*' Sarah jabbed a finger where Dixons had written the date on the poster. 'They've even stolen our pantomime day!'

Josie's heart sank. She'd felt so much happier since the subject of beating Dixons seemed to have been dropped. This would send it all kicking off again. 'Well, it's not their fault, is it? They don't know when we're doing the pantomime. We've only just arranged it.

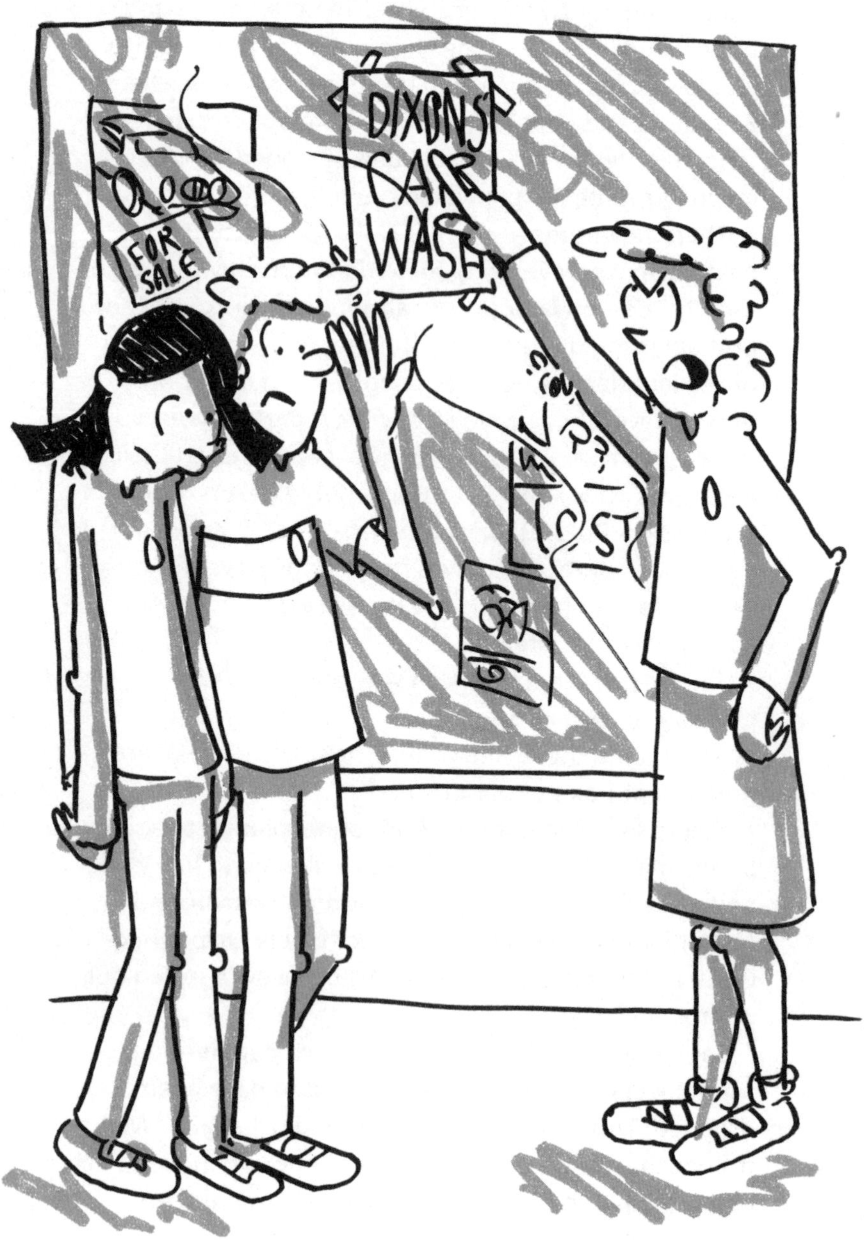
DIXONS' CAR WASH
FOR SALE
LOST

'And look,' she added, 'they *are* raising money for a charity. Hatherington House, see? So they are doing something good! And in any case, so what if they're washing cars on the same day as the panto? It's not really going to make any difference to us.'

'Of course it's going to make a difference to us!' Sarah shouted. 'People might decide to get their cars washed instead of coming to see *Cinderella*!'

Josie shook her head. 'They've got plenty of time to do both,' she said. 'Dixons are doing car-washing all day. We're not starting the pantomime until three o'clock.'

'Yes, but if they've given away all their money to Dixons in the morning,' Sarah argued, 'they're not going to have any left to buy a ticket to see *us*, are they?'

John made a face. 'Bit of an exaggeration, Sarah,' he muttered. He was beginning to feel uncomfortable that his sister was making such a fuss in the middle of the street. 'I'm sure people won't be giving *all* their money to Dixons. Besides, not everyone in the whole of Holly Hill's going to want to have their car washed! Not everyone in the whole of Holly Hill probably even *has* a car.'

'Yes, well you don't know anything, do you, John?' Sarah scowled. 'This is *my* pantomime and I'm not letting Dixons ruin it. We're going to go home and make our posters right now. And they're going to be much bigger and much more colourful than Dixons' rubbishy ones. Then no one will even *look* at their posters because they'll be so busy looking at ours! Are you coming, Josie?'

Josie didn't hesitate. 'No,' she said flatly.

Sarah stared at her. 'Josie,' she replied. 'Do you have any idea how important this competition is?'

'Yes!' Josie snapped. 'As a matter of fact, I do.

The trouble is, Sarah, that as far as you're concerned, it's important for all the wrong reasons!'

With that, she turned and marched away.

When Sarah arrived at church the next day, she had a stack of *Cinderella* posters with her. She'd spent hours getting them ready. They advertised: 'It's Panto and Picnic Time!' Sarah had written all the details using every colour of felt pen that she and John owned. She'd drawn a picture of a beautiful shoe on each one, too – the shoe Cinderella accidentally leaves behind when she runs away from the prince's party. For the pantomime itself, Sarah had decided to wear trainers to the party. But she'd jazzed them up by covering them with glue and giving them a hefty sprinkling of red and gold glitter.

'Oh,' said Danny when he saw the posters. 'I thought we were meeting tomorrow to make these.'

'We were,' replied Sarah. 'That was before I saw that Dixons had already put theirs up. I thought we should get ours out as quickly as possible. We can do it straight after Sunday Club. If we all put up a few, it won't take long.'

Sarah glanced at Josie, but Josie didn't look back at her. She didn't look at the posters either.

Just before the children left the service to go out to Sunday Club, Greg invited Topz up to the front of the church to tell everyone about the fundraising they were doing. Sarah had a little speech all worked out.

'We'll be selling tickets for the pantomime after church next Sunday,' she finished. 'Only £2.50 each! And all the money's going to *such* a great cause. Thank you very much!'

As she and the Gang turned to go, Josie suddenly stepped forwards. She knew she'd be in trouble with Topz for what she was about to do, but she couldn't stop herself. Greg was helping the Topz Gang by letting them advertise in church. Dixons could do with some help, too.

'Can I just say something, please?' Josie blurted out as quickly as she could. She gazed round at the congregation. Everyone was looking at her; waiting to hear what she had to say. There were so many faces that she almost lost her nerve. 'The pantomime's not the only charity event happening on that Saturday. There's also going to be car-washing in the community centre car park. You'll see posters around.'

Sarah had swung round and was gaping at her.

'It's to raise money for Hatherington House,' Josie gulped. 'The centre that helps people who've had strokes.'

That was it. That was all Josie wanted to say. But the whole church-full of people still had their eyes fixed on her, and she wasn't quite sure what she was meant to do next. Finally, she nodded her head, as if she was giving a brief bow, and hurried out to the hall.

Sarah caught up with her in seconds. The other Topz stood staring at the pair of them, frowning and looking confused.

'What did you do that for?' Sarah demanded. The shocked expression was still all over her face.

'What's this about car-washing?' asked Benny. 'What's it got to do with us?'

'Everything!' hissed Sarah. 'Dixons are doing it! They're trying to get everyone to go and get their cars washed instead of coming to see our pantomime!'

'No, they're not,' said John. 'We just saw one of

their posters yesterday. They happen to be doing their fundraising thing on the same day as we're doing ours, that's all.'

'Yes,' nodded Sarah. 'And now Josie's told the whole church about it.' She looked as if she might burst into tears.

'Yeah, why did you do that, Josie?' Benny demanded. 'All Dixons want to do is beat us in the competition, and you've just helped them out.'

Josie wanted so badly to be able to tell Topz why Dixons were supporting Hatherington House; why that particular charity was so special to Kevin. Then they'd understand. They'd think she'd done the right thing. Not Sarah, maybe, but the rest of the Gang would.

But Kevin had asked her not to so she couldn't say a word.

All she could do was shrug and murmur, 'Well, what's wrong with helping them? I think it's a really good charity to raise money for. So why shouldn't church know about it?'

Sarah didn't speak to Josie for the whole of Sunday Club. Every now and then, Josie tried to catch her eye. But Sarah was determined to ignore her, and in the end Josie gave up. If her best friend was going to be this petty, perhaps it wasn't worth being part of the pantomime. Clearly they both had completely different ideas about what was important. Maybe the best thing was for Josie to pull out now so that Sarah would have time to find someone else to play the fairy godmother. After all, Josie really wasn't interested any more.

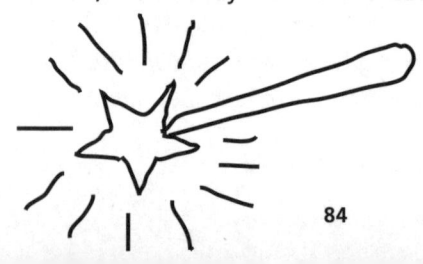

Eleven

Grandad was having a good day.

Kevin's mum had spent that Sunday morning cleaning his flat. She'd opened up the windows, scrubbed, hoovered, polished and put out the rubbish. Everywhere looked and smelt fresh.

When she stopped for a cup of coffee, she'd chatted with Grandad about the lovely weather and the busyness of Billings Road and what he might fancy to eat for his suppers this week. And Grandad had chatted back. He wasn't the least bit confused or forgetful today. Just the opposite. He seemed bright and cheerful and, for once, he had plenty to say.

Before Kevin's mum went home, she looked at him fondly. If only every day could be like today.

When she told Kevin how much better he seemed, Kevin couldn't help grinning.

'You see?' he said. 'I told you. He doesn't need to go into a care home. He's fine in his flat. Grandad's always all right. Besides,' he added, 'when I've finished doing this fundraising, Hatherington House will have more money. Then maybe Grandad will be able to go there sometimes. You know, for visits.'

A faint smile crossed his mum's lips, but it didn't show in her eyes. She wasn't going to tell Kevin that she'd already been to look at a few care homes in and around Holly Hill. She didn't mention that she'd found one where she thought Grandad might be happy. There was no point just yet. For the time being, there wasn't a room available there for Grandad. Why upset Kevin again before she had to?

As for telling Grandad himself, she planned to put it off for as long as she possibly could.

'I'll go round to see him,' Kevin said suddenly. 'If Grandad's feeling chatty, I'll go round there now. Keep him company. Maybe we'll even play chess.'

By the time Kevin was pressing on the buzzer at the main door of the flats, he'd decided against suggesting chess. He'd had a better idea.

'It's really warm and sunny out, Grandad. Let's go and sit in the garden, shall we?' he said. 'Under the window like we used to sometimes after school, remember?'

Grandad spluttered into a laugh. 'Of course I remember!' he replied. 'It wasn't that many years ago. But do you remember what I used to sit on?'

'Yeah! You've got a folding chair.'

'Exactly!' Grandad smiled. 'A very *low*, folding chair. And even if I can get myself into it, how precisely do you think I'm ever going to be able to get out of it?' He started chuckling again at the thought.

'Well, you don't have to use the folding chair, do you?' Kevin said. 'We'll just take a chair from the kitchen.'

It felt a little strange to both of them, sitting outside at the front of the flats. They hadn't done it for so long. Grandad settled himself somewhat stiffly onto the kitchen chair Kevin had carried out for him. Kevin perched on the same folding stool he'd sat on years ago. He felt too big for it now. It wobbled underneath him.

'Busy,' remarked Grandad, nodding towards Billings Road.

Car after car swept past the lines of vehicles already parked down each side of the street.

'Shall we play that guessing game?' Kevin asked. 'Guess the colour of the next car to come past?'

'If you like,' smiled Grandad. Kevin might have grown older – he might spend too much time with the wrong sort of kids – but he hadn't forgotten, Grandad thought. He still remembered the special times they'd shared on the days when Grandad picked him up from Holly Hill School. Perhaps he always would.

'Blue!' cried Kevin. A red car drove into view. 'Aww! Your turn, Grandad.'

'Silver,' said Grandad. The next car to drive past was black.

'Black, then,' laughed Kevin. But the car that was next to drive along Billings Road was white.

After a while, as the afternoon sun beat down, Kevin did guess right. Red, and a red car glided past. Grandad guessed a couple right, too. But they hadn't been playing long when Kevin heard him sigh.

'What's wrong, Grandad?' he asked. 'We can stop if you want.'

Grandad nodded. 'Yes,' he mumbled. 'Yes, I think I would like to stop now. Would you mind if we went back inside, Kevin? That sun's a little too hot for me.'

Kevin put the chair back in the kitchen and tucked the folding stool into the cupboard in the hallway. He put the kettle on and made Grandad a cup of tea. And when he saw his grandad's eyes beginning to droop sleepily, Kevin said, 'I'll get going then. Mum'll be round later with your supper. See you soon, eh, Grandad?'

Outside again, Kevin paused as the main entrance door to the flats swung closed. He was glad he'd gone to visit. He was glad he and Grandad had sat outside together in the sunshine, the way they used to, chatting, guessing car colours.

But he was sad, too.
Grandad seemed so old.

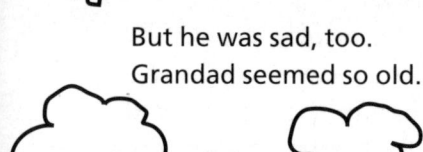

After Sunday Club, Sarah, John, Danny and Benny had wandered around Holly Hill with Sarah's posters. Just like Dixons, they'd managed to get some into shop windows and doors. Mr Smithson had said they were welcome to put one on the noticeboard outside the school, too. It was a bit of a walk from the shopping centre, but Sarah had made a special poster for there and she wanted to get it pinned up. Instead of advertising that the pantomime would be performed at the school playing field, Sarah had written across the top of this one, in big red letters: OPEN-AIR PANTOMIME HERE!

Once it was in place on the noticeboard, she stood back to look at it.

'What do you think?' she asked the others. 'Can you see it?'

'Of course we can see it!' said John.

'No,' replied Sarah, 'I mean, can you *really* see it? If you were driving along the road in a car, would you be able to see it then?'

Benny burst out laughing. 'I hope not! If I was driving along the road in a car, I hope I'd be watching the road!'

Sarah raised her eyes. 'Oh, you know what I mean,' she persisted. 'Will people notice it? We need them to be able to see instantly that something really interesting's going on here.'

The boys glanced at each other.

'It's a good poster,' Danny shrugged. 'Stop worrying,

Sarah. People will notice.'

Sarah still had several posters left, but by now the four of them were starving. They'd gone straight out after Sunday Club, so they hadn't had any lunch.

'I've got to go home and get food,' said Benny. 'Can we do some more later?'

'That's OK,' said Sarah. 'I can finish doing these.'

As they'd gone from shop to shop, then walked back through Holly Hill to the school, Sarah had noticed several of Dixons' posters. Some of them were in shop windows. There was nothing she could do about those.

Some of them, however, were on lampposts. They were stuck there with tape. The chances were, they'd fall off the next time it rained. But Sarah had decided not to leave it to a possible shower to get rid of Dixons' posters. She'd made up her mind to do it herself.

When she and John got home, she ate her lunch quickly.

'Off again?' asked her mum.

'I just want to get the rest of these posters up,' she smiled.

'I'll come with you, if you like,' John said. 'I can bring Gruff. I need to take him for a walk anyway.'

Sarah shook her head. 'No, that's OK. I'm only going to be walking round the roads. Take him to the park. He likes that better.'

With the pantomime posters and some of her dad's wide, sticky tape from his toolbox in a carrier bag, Sarah hurried off back towards the shopping centre. There was a lamppost by one of the bus stops along the main road where she'd seen a Dixons poster. That was where she headed first.

As she got closer, she could see there was no one

waiting at the stop. In fact, apart from the cars driving up and down, there was hardly anyone about at all. It was perfect! She could tear the Dixons poster down and stick one up for *Cinderella* with no one there to take notice of what she was doing.

Standing in front of the lamppost, Sarah glanced around her once more. Her breathing quickened. She knew she shouldn't do what she was about to do. She knew it was wrong. But that didn't stop her.

Dropping the carrier bag onto the pavement, quickly her hands shot out and ripped at the poster Dixons had stuck there advertising their car-wash. The tape didn't come away as easily as she thought it would. She had to scrabble at it with her fingernails. Her eyes kept darting about her all the time. Was anyone looking? Had anyone seen?

Finally, she managed to tear it down. She screwed it up into a tight ball, picked up the carrier bag and dropped it inside. Then she took the tape and one of her own posters, and stuck that up on the lamppost instead.

Sarah didn't stop to inspect her handiwork as she had outside school. This time, as soon as she'd finished, she scurried away. She couldn't afford to be spotted there. She felt breathless. Her heart was thudding a little in her chest, but she'd done it! She'd got rid of a Dixons poster and replaced it with one of Topz's. Anyone passing that particular lamppost would now know all about the pantomime and nothing about the car-washing at the community centre.

But Sarah wasn't finished. There were three more posters in the bag and she planned to do the same thing three more times.

It wasn't so easy closer to the shopping centre. There were more people around. In some ways, Sarah supposed it didn't really matter if she *was* seen. People took down posters and put up new ones all the time. Probably no one would take any notice. Except that Sarah was doing something she knew she shouldn't be. So she couldn't help feeling that other people would know it, too.

At last, she had just one poster left. She remembered seeing another one of Dixons' just up the road on the other side. It was stuck up on the lamppost in front of the bingo hall. She crossed over and made her way towards it.

Once again she reached up and scratched away at the tape with her fingernails. Once again she ripped the Dixons poster down and scrunched it into a ball. Once more, Sarah thought she'd got away with it.

She was wrong.
'Oi!'
Sarah was so startled, she dropped the ball of paper onto the pavement. It rolled over the kerb into the gutter.

'What do you think you're doing? **That's one of our posters!'**

All of a sudden, Kevin was standing right in front of her. His fists were clenched and his eyes glared.

Sarah stared back at him, frozen to the spot.

Twelve

First, Kevin bent down and snatched the ruined poster out of the gutter.

Next, he grabbed Sarah's carrier bag and looked inside, where he spotted the other three tightly scrunched balls of paper. He didn't have to open them up to know they were more of Dixons' posters.

He noticed the remaining pantomime poster, too, along with the roll of tape. It was perfectly clear to him what Sarah was about to do.

Sarah could hardly breathe. If she thought her heart was thumping before, now it seemed to be trying to burst out of her chest. She looked into Kevin's face, absolutely terrified. You didn't mess with Dixons! Just about every kid in Holly Hill knew that. The Topz Gang more than any of them!

Not only had Sarah just messed with them really badly, but she knew she was in the wrong.

'Do you want to know what it feels like?' Kevin snarled. 'Do you?'

He tore the Topz poster from the bag. His face twisted viciously as he glanced at it.

'It's rubbish!' he yelled. 'Rick's right! Your pantomime idea *is* soppy! Do you really think you're going to make money out of some sad, pathetic, *Topzy* version of sad, pathetic *Cinderella*?'

Sarah couldn't speak. She was too scared.

'Well, do you?' Kevin hissed. 'Because you won't! You won't raise a thing! I'm going to take down all your posters. No one will know anything about your pantomime. And anyone who does know won't want to go anyway!'

With that, he dropped the carrier bag, ripped Sarah's last poster to pieces and hurled them in her face. 'And don't you ever,' he growled, '*ever* pretend that you Topz care about anyone but yourselves. Because I know different now, don't I?'

Sarah couldn't look at him any more. And she didn't want Kevin looking at her any more either. Suddenly, it hit her! What had she done? As if it wasn't bad enough that she'd destroyed some of Dixons' posters, she'd let Topz down. Worse than that – much worse – she'd let God down. As Kevin stood there scowling at her, he didn't see anything of God in her, did he? All he saw was a nasty girl who'd set out to spoil Dixons' hard work.

Sarah turned and ran. Her mind raced, along with her feet. She had to get away from there. She had to get home where she'd be safe. Kevin might come after her. If he caught up with her, what would he do …?

But, as scary as that thought was, there was something else, far bigger, now pounding through Sarah's brain as she ran. Questions she couldn't escape: What did God think of her right now? And what would Topz say when they found out what she'd done?

Josie hated falling out with Sarah. It made her whole world feel wrong. She wished so much that there wasn't a fundraising competition. Or at least that the Topz Gang weren't taking part in it. The pantomime would have been such fun if it had had nothing to do with winning or losing.

When Josie got home after Sunday Club, she wasn't sure what to do. She hadn't wanted to join in with the others putting posters up around Holly Hill. But as the afternoon ticked by, she began to feel she should have gone with them anyway. It was horrible not talking to Sarah. Josie wondered whether she should go round to see her. But supposing Sarah was still cross with her for advertising Dixons' car-washing event in church? If she was, Josie would be the last person she'd want to see.

Instead, Josie decided to take her script to the park. The afternoon was hot and sunny. She'd rather be outside. And however she felt about the pantomime, she had to try to learn her words. In any case, she might bump into Sarah down there. Then her best friend would see she was working on the script and perhaps that would put everything right between them again.

Josie was in no particular hurry, so she walked slowly. She was just about to cross the road opposite the park gates when a yell behind her made her turn sharply.

'Hey you! Topzy!'

Kevin was marching towards her.

'How *could* you?' he shouted.

Josie looked at him blankly, but as he reached her, he didn't give her a chance to speak.

'You know how important this fundraising is to me!' he muttered, teeth clenched together. 'I told you why! I haven't told anyone else, but I told you. And you go and do *this*!'

Kevin tipped the bag he was carrying upside down. Out fell what looked like rubbish. Screwed up paper.

Josie stared at it, then her eyes shot back to Kevin, searching his face. She didn't like this. She was frightened. The last kid in the whole of Holly Hill you'd want to get on the wrong side of was a Dixon. But Kevin seemed furious with her and she had no idea why.

She shook her head. 'What is it, Kevin?' she asked nervously. 'I don't know what I've done. What's this?' Josie indicated the rubbish on the pavement.

'Have a look,' muttered Kevin. 'Go on, have a look!'

Slowly, Josie bent down, picked up one of the paper balls and carefully unscrewed it. Still, nothing made sense. 'I don't understand,' she mumbled. 'It's one of your posters. Why have you screwed them up?'

'*I* didn't screw them up, did I?' Kevin snapped. '*I've* been sticking them round Holly Hill. It's you Topzies who've been taking them down!'

Josie looked horrified. 'We haven't!' she cried. 'We wouldn't! We'd *never* do anything like that!'

'Oh yeah?' retorted Kevin. 'Well, guess what? I know you did do it, and do you want to know *how* I know? Because I saw your mate, Sarah! She's been ripping these down and sticking your Topz ones up instead!'

Josie didn't reply. She just kept staring into Kevin's face. She wanted to shout, 'You're wrong! You're lying!' But as she gazed at him, she knew he wasn't. She knew he was telling the truth.

'I'm sorry.' Josie spoke in barely a whisper. 'I'm so sorry, Kevin. I didn't know. I know you'll never believe me now, but I honestly didn't know.'

'Of course you knew!' Kevin hissed. 'I told you why I wanted to be in the competition; why I wanted to raise some money. I told you why my charity's important. But you don't care, do you? You all pretend to be so "nice", but you don't actually care about anyone! All you want to do is win! Well, it's never going to happen, Josie!' he shouted, thrusting his face close to hers.

'I didn't care about winning or losing when this started, but I do now. And Dixons are going to beat Topz in this competition! We're going to raise more money than you because we'll make sure that no one – NO ONE – goes anywhere near your stupid pantomime!'

As suddenly as Kevin had appeared, he was gone.

Josie looked down. The bag and the screwed up posters still lay by her feet. Slowly she bent down to pick them up.

What had Sarah done? How could she? Kevin had trusted Josie enough to tell her a secret; enough to talk to her about his grandad. She hadn't told anyone. He'd asked her not to and she hadn't said a word. But because of Sarah, he still thought she'd betrayed him.

Clutching the carrier bag and the notebook, Josie set off back home. She'd gone off the whole idea of learning her fairy godmother words in the park. In fact, she wasn't interested in learning her script anywhere.

When she got to her street, she hesitated. Then she made a decision. She didn't head up towards the flats where she lived. Instead she carried straight on, turning left when she reached the bottom of the hill.

This was Sarah's road. In a few more moments, Josie was knocking at her door.

Sarah's mum answered.

'Hello, Josie,' she smiled. 'Come on in.'

Josie shook her head. 'No, that's OK, thanks. I can't stop. Could I just see Sarah for a minute, please? I've got something for her.'

'Of course, you can,' replied Sarah's mum. 'I'll go and get her. But you can still wait inside, you know.'

Again, Josie shook her head. 'No. Thanks.'

When Sarah appeared, she didn't seem the way Josie

expected her to. Josie imagined Sarah would look smug. Pleased with herself because, now she'd got rid of some of Dixons' posters, she was one step closer to beating them in the competition. Instead, she looked pale, Josie thought. Worried. Any other day Josie would have asked her if she was all right.

But this wasn't any other day.

'Hi, Josie. You OK?' Sarah said quietly.

'No, I'm not,' Josie answered.

Without another word, she held out the carrier bag. Sarah took it slowly. It was the same bag she'd dropped by the bingo hall. She didn't need to look inside to know that Dixons' posters were in there.

'Where did you find them?' she gulped.

Josie shrugged. 'I saw Kevin. He's really angry, Sarah. He thinks this is down to all of us. All of Topz.' She paused, pressing her lips together tightly. 'Kevin told me something,' she went on finally. 'He trusted me enough to tell me something he didn't want anyone else to know. Now, thanks to you, he'll never trust me again.'

'Josie –' Sarah began.

But Josie wasn't interested in anything her friend had to say. This time, she held out the notebook with all her script for the pantomime written in it.

'You can have this back,' she murmured. 'I don't want it any more. You'd better find yourself a new fairy godmother. And while you're about it,' she added, the words beginning to catch in her throat as tears suddenly sprang into her eyes, **'you may as well find yourself a new best friend!'**

Thirteen

Sarah left the house early.

'Where are you off to first thing on a holiday morning?' her mum asked.

'Nowhere really,' Sarah shrugged. She pointed to the carrier bag in her hand. 'I've just got some more posters to put up. I won't be long.'

Sarah didn't say 'pantomime' posters. That's because the posters in the bag were nothing to do with the pantomime.

After Josie had left the day before, Sarah had disappeared to her room, curled up on her bed and lain there, sobbing. It was terrible what she'd done to Dixons. She could hardly believe she'd let herself behave like that. Dixons would never forget it and, more than likely, nor would Topz when they found out.

They *would* find out, too. Josie would tell them. Even if she didn't, Kevin was bound to confront them sooner or later. In any case, there was a pantomime rehearsal that afternoon. She was sure Dave wouldn't mind playing the fairy godmother (they could easily change it to a fairy godfather). But she'd still have to explain why Josie didn't want to have anything to do with it any more.

As Sarah lay on the bed, she told God she was sorry, over and over again. But how could she make things right with Josie? And how could she show Dixons that she wished with all her heart she'd left their posters alone?

That's when the idea came to her. There was something she could do. It might not make the slightest difference to the way Dixons felt. On the other hand, maybe it would be just enough to show them that she really was sorry.

Sarah rolled off the bed. From underneath it, she pulled the carrier bag with Dixons' scrunched up posters inside. She'd stuffed it there after Josie had given it to her. Smoothing out one of the posters, she put it on her desk. Then, using paper left over from the *Cinderella* posters, she began to make new ones advertising Dixons' car-wash.

Sarah copied all the details from the poster Kevin had made. She even kept to just black felt tip, exactly as Kevin had done. Although she would have liked to use a rainbow of colours to make the posters really stand out, she didn't think that's what Dixons would want.

Sarah managed to make nine car-wash posters before she ran out of paper. That was more than twice the number she'd taken down. Now what she had to do was go around Holly Hill and replace the four she'd got rid of, if Dixons hadn't done it already. She'd also find five more lampposts for the posters she had left over. She'd do it first thing in the morning.

When she'd finished, there was one more thing Sarah needed to do. The thought of it scared her but that didn't matter. Fear couldn't stop her. She had to talk to Dixons. As often as not, they were in the park. If she went there and waited for them after she'd put all the posters out, she was sure they'd turn up …

The first thing Sarah noticed when she went out early that morning was that every single Topz poster was gone from the lampposts in Holly Hill. Not just the ones where they'd replaced car-washing posters – they were gone from all of them. Sarah had half-expected that. But now the lampposts were empty. Dixons obviously hadn't got round to making new posters because they hadn't put anything up in place of the ones they'd torn down. So Sarah set to work.

Putting the posters up was the easy part. Waiting for Dixons to turn up in the park so that she could talk to them was much, much harder. Would they even listen to her? And if they did, would they believe what she had to say?

Sarah sat on one of the swings, rocking herself backwards and forwards. She desperately wanted Dixons to appear but at the same time she hoped they wouldn't. Every so often, she stood up and had a good look all around. Perhaps they were in the park already and she just hadn't noticed them. But, no, there was no sign of them. So she went back to rocking slowly on the swing. Fortunately there was no sign of any of the Topz Gang either. Sarah wasn't ready to bump into them. Not yet. Not till she'd spoken to Dixons.

When at last the Dixons Gang did show up, Sarah heard them before she saw them. Rick, Kevin and Clyde rolled loudly in through the park gates on their skateboards. Kevin stopped abruptly when he spotted the Topz girl. He watched with a face like thunder as she got slowly to her feet and began to walk towards them.

'Well, look who it is,' grunted Rick nastily. 'The little girl who can't keep her hands off other people's posters.'

'I need to talk to you,' Sarah mumbled.

'What?' Rick cupped a hand to his ear. 'Sorry, did anyone else hear something?'

'Yeah,' muttered Clyde. 'Something horrible and squeaky.'

The only one who didn't say a word was Kevin.

Sarah licked her lips nervously. This was going to be even tougher than she'd thought.

'Look,' she began again. 'You can make fun of me or be nasty to me, or anything you want. It's not like I don't deserve it. But I really need you to listen to me first.'

'Yeah?' Clyde growled. 'Well, you've got nothing to say that we want to hear.'

'Too right,' said Rick. 'I thought your pantomime idea was pathetic, but it's got nothing on you.'

He started to push forward again on his skateboard. The other two boys followed. Clyde and Kevin deliberately shoved into her as they passed by her on the path.

Sarah twisted round.

'Fine!' she shouted after them. 'But I'm going to tell you what I've got to say, whether you listen to me or not! Topz didn't know anything about your posters! It was me! I took them down on my own! I didn't tell anyone. I probably *wouldn't* have told anyone, either. Not if you hadn't caught me, Kevin.'

She paused. The three boys weren't looking at her but they'd stopped skateboarding. She was fairly sure she had their attention.

'I feel awful!' she gulped. 'It feels like the worst thing I've ever done. So you can believe me or not, but I'm really, *really* sorry and I wish it had never happened. But please, please don't blame Topz. It had nothing to do with them. In fact, when they find out, they'll probably hate me as much as you do.'

Kevin was the first of the three to turn back. As he did so, his eye seemed to be caught by something behind her.

'OK,' he nodded. 'Well, let's find out, shall we?'

Sarah frowned. What did he mean? What was he looking at?

'You all right, Sarah? What's up?'

Sarah groaned inwardly. Just when it felt as though things couldn't get any worse, suddenly they had.

Danny was standing right behind her. He had a football with him. He was probably looking for someone to have a kickabout with.

'Go on, then,' Kevin said. 'Tell him. Let's see how much he hates you.'

Danny frowned. 'Tell me what?'

Sarah bit her lip. Josie knew about the posters. Did another Topz really have to find out here and now? In front of the Dixons Gang?

'Tell me what?' Danny repeated. 'Sarah?'

'Well, go on,' Kevin grunted spitefully.

Tiredly, Sarah sighed. 'I took down some of the car-washing posters and put *Cinderella* ones up instead.'

'What are you talking about?' Danny asked. 'We put the posters up together. You didn't touch any of theirs.'

Sarah nodded. 'Yes, I did. I went back out later.'

Danny stared at her for a moment. It was hard to grasp what she was saying. Sarah could be silly and bossy and annoying, but she wasn't mean. Taking down Dixons' posters was a mean thing to do. Danny couldn't quite believe it.

Sarah hung her head. 'I came to the park to say sorry,' she said quietly. 'I don't know why I did it. Josie told me the fundraising shouldn't be about winning and losing. I didn't listen to her. I still wanted Topz to win.'

Kevin was watching Danny closely. The Topz boy looked so confused that perhaps Sarah *was* telling the truth. Maybe the other Topz *didn't* know about the posters.

But that didn't change what she'd done.

Kevin's gaze flicked back to Sarah. Her eyes were swimming with tears.

'Well, she's said she's sorry,' Danny said suddenly. 'We all do stuff sometimes, don't we?'

Rick and Clyde exchanged a look. 'Come on, Kev,' muttered Clyde. 'We don't have to listen to this.'

Kevin stood there for one more short moment before he turned to head off with the others.

'Anyway, I made you new posters!' Sarah blurted out.

Tears were trickling down her face and she brushed them away angrily.

'Yeah, sure you did,' sneered Rick over his shoulder.

'I did! I put them up on lots of lampposts,' Sarah shouted after them. 'You'll see them if you go down through the shopping centre.'

'But we're not going to the shopping centre, are we?' yelled Clyde. 'Like we're going to believe anything you say anyway!'

Sarah stared after them miserably. They didn't say another word. They didn't turn back.

A minute or so passed before Danny gave her a nudge.

'You all right?' he asked.

Sarah didn't look at him. She just shook her head and walked out of the park.

Fourteen

The day before Topz's pantomime and Dixons' big car-wash event, Kevin was in a good mood.

He'd spent the previous afternoon at the supermarket, packing bags with Rick and Clyde. When they counted up all the coins in their donation buckets, they came to just over eighty pounds!

'If we can at least double that with the cars we wash,' Clyde grinned, 'then we'll win this contest no problem!'

'Yeah!' crowed Rick. 'And Topz will be the losers! Serve them right, too.'

Dixons had found the posters Sarah had put up for them. Anyone could see she was sorry. But that didn't change how they felt about the Topz Gang or beating them in the competition.

Kevin was pleased with how well they'd done at the supermarket, too. But not because of Topz. He still hadn't told Dixons why he'd chosen Hatherington House as their charity. He was just glad they might end up with a decent amount of money to donate.

He was in the kitchen, putting the sponges and car shampoo for the following day's car-wash into a bucket, when the phone rang.

'Get that, would you, Kevin?' his stepdad called through from the lounge.

The Dixons boy picked up the receiver.

'Kevin?' It was his mum. She sounded flustered. 'Grandad's not here.'

Kevin's mum had taken the afternoon off work. She'd popped home for lunch. Then she'd gone straight out again to get Grandad some shopping and take it round to him at the flat.

Kevin thought for a moment. 'Well ... maybe he's gone out for a walk.'

'I told him I was coming over, Kevin,' his mum replied snappily.

'Yes, but he might have forgotten. Maybe he's having one of those days.'

'No,' his mum insisted. 'He knows well enough he's not to go out on his own. It's not safe for him.'

'What about Mrs Rawlings?' Kevin answered. 'I bet she knows where he is. She's good at keeping an eye on him.'

'No,' said his mum again. 'I've spoken to her. She hasn't seen him since she popped down here early this morning. She says she was quite worried about him, too. He was a bit vague and anxious apparently. She said she was going to call me if he didn't seem better this afternoon.'

Kevin sighed. His good mood vanished. Now all he felt was worry, and he didn't want that.

'OK,' he muttered. 'Do you want me to go looking?'

'Please,' said his mum. 'I'm going to try all round the shopping centre. I'm hoping he's got his phone with him. I can't find it anywhere in the flat. I've tried ringing it but he hasn't got it switched on. Either that or he's out of battery. Anyway, if you find him before I do, ask him for his phone and ring me on my mobile straightaway. You got that? Straightaway, Kevin.'

Kevin hurried out of the house.

'Who was that?' Mike called as his stepson opened the front door.

'Mum. She can't find Grandad.'

'What, again?' was all Mike replied.

And Kevin was gone.

The shopping centre was the obvious place to look first, but that's where his mum was going. There was no point in them both searching the same area. So where should he start? Grandad wouldn't have gone far, would he? Walking wasn't easy for him. It was a hot day, too. He'd get tired quickly.

Kevin stopped at the end of his road. His mind was racing. 'Come on, think!' he muttered to himself.

But nothing came to him. No ideas as to where his grandad might head for.

In the end, all he could think to do was to go to the park and work his way up through Holly Hill from there. Maybe Kevin would find him at the tennis courts. Grandad had loved the times when Kevin was small and they'd gone there after school to knock a ball about. He used to enjoy watching other people playing, too. Perhaps that's what he'd decided to do this afternoon. After all, it was a perfect summer's day …

'That's it,' said Benny. 'That's the last time we're doing it till we have crowds of people watching!'

Topz were on Holly Hill School's playing field. They'd just completed their last *Cinderella* rehearsal before their performance the following day. They were all wearing their costumes and they were boiling hot! Especially Cinderella's wicked stepmother (Paul) and her two stepsisters (Benny and John).

'I'm stifling in this wig,' moaned Paul, grasping it in a hot, sticky hand and pulling it off.

'Me, too,' agreed John. He dragged his own wig off and fanned his face with it.

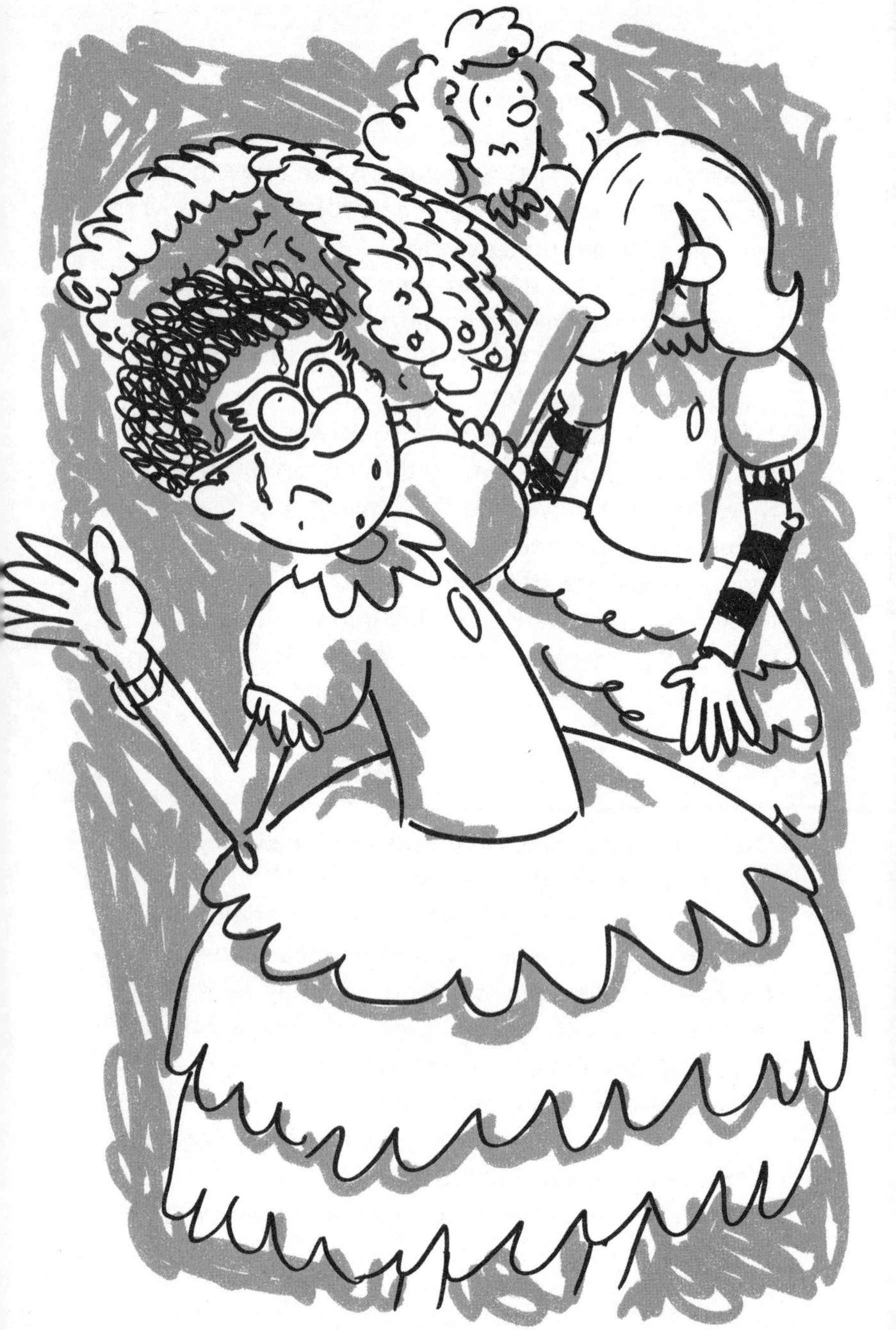

'Yes, but you look perfect!' beamed Sarah. 'Everyone looks perfect! And it was all OK, wasn't it, Dave?' she asked, glancing across at him.

Dave, the pantomime director, had been sitting on the grass, watching. Mr Smithson, the school caretaker, was there, too. He'd come over that afternoon to unlock the school gate and let them in.

'It was brilliant!' Dave grinned, getting to his feet and brushing grass from his jeans. 'And I know it was my idea, but my favourite bit's still where the fairy godmother turns that butternut squash into a bicycle!'

Topz had had to make a few changes to the *Cinderella* story. They couldn't find a pumpkin for Cinderella's godmother to turn into a coach, so they'd decided to use a large butternut squash instead. As for the coach itself, they hadn't had time to build anything complicated, so Dave had suggested a bike. Sarah loved the idea. When Topz' Cinderella went off to the party, she cycled!

'Can you help me off with my wings, please, Sarah?'

Sarah turned. Josie was standing behind her, struggling to get her arms out of the elastic that held the wings she'd made in place on her back.

In the end, Sarah hadn't had to find another fairy godmother.

She hadn't had to find a new best friend either.

Danny had told Josie what had happened in the park. How Sarah had said sorry to Dixons for taking their posters down; how she'd made them a set of new posters and gone around Holly Hill putting them up.

When the two girls next saw each other, it was Josie who was the sorry one. Sarah just smiled and shrugged and told her she'd been right to be cross.

'It was me, not you. I did get everything round the wrong way,' Sarah said. 'I wanted to win the competition because the pantomime was my idea and Dixons thought it was stupid. As soon as they said that, I forgot about what was important – about raising money to help a charity. I just wanted to beat them. It was like you said, I pushed God totally out of it.'

Standing on the playing field in her fairy godmother outfit, Josie turned, held her arms straight out behind her and Sarah carefully pulled the wings off.

Josie was about to turn back again when she spotted someone sitting on the bench outside the school gate.

'What is it?' Sarah asked.

Josie nodded towards the bench. 'Do you think people have started queuing for the pantomime already?'

The girls laughed, but as Josie squinted across the field in the sunshine, she suddenly realised who it was.

She took a few steps nearer.

'Isn't that …?' she began.

'Who?' Sarah was peering now, too.

'I think it's Kevin's grandad. We met him, remember? A couple of weeks ago when we were at the shopping centre buying notebooks.'

Sarah looked more closely. 'It could be him,' she nodded. 'Yes, I think it is.'

'What's he doing here?' Josie wondered.

'Maybe he's out for a walk and just wanted a sit down,' answered Sarah.

'But he's not supposed to be out on his own,' frowned Josie. 'Kevin told me.'

Leaving the other Topz to start packing up, Josie and Sarah ran down to the school gate.

The elderly man sitting on the bench didn't seem to

notice them. Not until Josie spoke.

'Hello. You're Kevin's grandad, aren't you? Is everything all right?'

Grandad turned his head a little to look at her. 'Not really,' he said. 'School must be late finishing today. Kevin should be out by now. I've been waiting for him for ages.'

Josie and Sarah glanced at each other. Neither of them quite knew what to say.

'Erm ...' Josie began finally. 'It's the holidays. School isn't on today.'

'And Kevin doesn't go to this school any more,' added Sarah. 'He goes to Southlands now. Do you know where that is?'

'Southlands?' Grandad said. 'What's Southlands? And where's Kevin? I told his mum I'd pick him up today. I can't go home without him.'

Kevin had told Josie a little about his grandad the day she'd bumped into him under the trees next to the football field. He'd told her how he got confused sometimes. This must be a confused day.

'I tell you what,' said Josie gently, sitting down on the bench next to him. 'My friend, Sarah, will go and have a look for Kevin.' Josie glanced up at Sarah as she spoke.

Sarah frowned. The idea of having to go and find a Dixon wasn't very appealing. Especially Kevin. He hated her now even more than he used to, she was sure of it.

Josie didn't take her eyes from Sarah's. 'I'm sure Sarah will find him, won't you, Sarah?' she went on. 'And I'll stay here and keep you company till she gets back.'

There was nothing for it. Reluctantly, Sarah had to agree. She raced back up to the playing field. After a few moments, she returned with Dave and Mr Smithson.

If Dave went with her to try to find Kevin, it might not be quite so awkward.

Mr Smithson sat on the bench with Grandad and Josie. They talked about lots of different things: the beautiful weather; Topz's summer pantomime; how lucky the children at Holly Hill Primary School were to have their very own playing field.

But mostly what Grandad talked about was Kevin.

'He's a good boy,' Grandad said. 'I'm teaching him to play tennis, you know. I reckon he's got a real talent for it. He's got a strong right arm. And a real appetite for buttered crumpets! Yes,' he nodded. 'He'll be all right at tennis will young Kevin. Just got to keep him on the straight and narrow.'

Topz had finished packing away after their rehearsal and were waiting at the gate with Josie when, almost an hour later, Sarah and Dave arrived back at the school. Kevin and his mum were with them. His mum had driven them all in the car.

As Kevin and Mr Smithson helped Grandad up and into the front seat, Kevin's mum turned to the Topz Gang.

'Thank you,' she said. 'Thanks for looking after him.'

Kevin didn't really look at them. As soon as Grandad was in the car, he slid into the back seat. Then his mum climbed in next to Grandad and drove away.

Fifteen

When the summer holidays were over, Josie didn't mind going back to school. Most of the time, she was happy there. And the start of this particular term would be exciting. It meant finding out which team had won the fundraising competition.

Josie still didn't mind whether Topz won or lost. Neither did Sarah any more. But they were both curious as to how much money they'd raised compared to everyone else. They also wanted to hear about other teams and the different ideas they'd had for fundraising.

The Topz pantomime had been a huge success, even though in the end things hadn't quite gone to plan. The morning of their performance day had been dry and sunny. Perfect picnic and pantomime weather, Sarah said.

But as the day wore on, the dark clouds had gradually rolled in. An hour before the performance was due to start, the rain began. It wasn't a fine, mizzly rain either. It was heavy and persistent, and there was no sign of it passing over.

Fortunately for Topz, Mr Smithson was prepared for anything. He'd already spoken to the head teacher about allowing Topz to use the school hall should the weather change. And the audience that started to arrive with picnic baskets and blankets were just as happy to spread themselves out on the wooden hall floor as they would have been on the grass.

Plenty of people turned up for Dixons' car-washing, too. And as they were ready for customers at the community centre in the morning before the bad weather came, it didn't really affect them either.

The competition results weren't announced in assembly at Holly Hill and Southlands Schools until the second week of term. When the day came, what surprised and delighted Josie wasn't so much that, out of all the teams that entered, it was Topz who came first, with Dixons a close second. It wasn't even that the promised afternoon at the quad bike centre for the winners was to be very soon – on the Saturday after next.

The most amazing thing as far as Josie was concerned was what happened after school on the day of the announcement.

I can't stop thinking about that verse in Matthew in the Bible, God: '... be concerned above everything else with the Kingdom of God and with what he requires of you ...' My mind keeps going over and over it. The most important thing is to put You first. In everything. If we can do that then we'll be living our lives the way You want us to; the way You **designed** *us to.*

But it's hard when we want to do stuff **our** *way. Or when we just want to do things that You might not want us to. Greg says that a lot of the time, all we want to do is to put* **ourselves** *first. So that's what we do. It's easier and we think it'll make us happy.*

Well, do You know what, God? There's not much that could make me happier than I am right now! And it's got nothing to do with me and everything to do with You being in first place! Although, actually, I suppose it is to do with someone else as well. Two people, really ... No, three.

The first one is Kevin. He gets in trouble a lot. He's a bit of a bully. All of Dixons are. But Kevin showed me something, God. Something I never thought I'd see. You knew it was there, though, didn't You? That day when he told me about Hatherington House and why he wanted to raise some money for it, he showed me that he can be loving. Kevin cares so much about his grandad and what's happening to him. That was the most important thing to him about the competition. He wasn't bothered about beating us Topz, was he? All he wanted to do was help people like his grandad.

The second person **is** *Kevin's grandad. He's not very well, God. Kevin says it's not just because of his stroke. He has something else going on in his brain now, too. That's why he gets confused and can't always remember where he is or what he's supposed to be doing. And once – only once, but Kevin says it'll probably happen again – his grandad didn't even recognise him. Just for a second he didn't know who Kevin was. That must have been so horrible for Kevin.*

And it must be so horrible for his grandad to know that he's not well and not able to cope on his own the way he used to. Kevin says he's probably going to have to go and live in a special home where people with his sorts of problems can be properly looked after. First of all Kevin didn't want him to have to move out of his flat. But then his grandad wandered off that day we found him outside school, and now Kevin knows he can't be left on his own to do that again.

So Kevin's been and visited a care home that his mum

found, and he says it's probably better for his grandad to live there. Then he'll be safe and comfortable. Until he moves into the home, though, he's going to go to Hatherington House sometimes for day care. Isn't that fantastic, God? Dixons raised money for Hatherington and Kevin's grandad's going to be looked after there!

Then there's the third person who's part of this just INCREDIBLE story. It's my best friend, Sarah. We had such a bad argument in the holidays. I wanted our fundraising to be all about You, God. I wanted You to be right in the middle of it so that You could help us to do the best we could with the pantomime and raise as much money for the rescue centre as possible. But all Sarah could think about for ages was beating Dixons. Trying to be better than they are. And it all went wrong, God.

Until Sarah listened to You.

*She knew she'd done something bad by taking down Dixons' posters, so she said sorry and she made even **better** and even **more** posters for them. She did everything she could to show them that she wished she'd never done it. Dixons didn't say anything, but they must have realised. And what's so amazing, God, is that if that bad thing hadn't happened then other things might not have changed. You still might not have been at the centre. It was only when Sarah realised what she'd done that she understood what I'd been trying to say. Then Sarah wanted to put You first in our fundraising, too.*

And by putting You first, God, something even more INCREDIBLE has happened! After school today, Sarah asked me if I'd wait in the park with her. She said she wanted to see Kevin. She wouldn't tell me why, though. She just said I'd find out if we bumped into him.

Well, I was dying to know, wasn't I? I was a bit scared, too. After all, we were the winners and Dixons weren't. I thought they might be really annoyed with us. Anyway, Topz don't hang around waiting to bump into Dixons. It's just not what we do.

But we did bump into Kevin. Well, not bump into him exactly. Sarah spotted him over the road from the park coming out of the newsagents. He was on his own, too, which was brilliant. I don't know where Rick and Clyde were. So Sarah marched straight over to him.

'I'm sorry you didn't win the competition, Kevin,' she said.

Kevin looked so surprised. I must have looked pretty surprised myself!

'Anyway, I've checked it out with most of Topz and ...' Sarah paused for a second and looked at me. 'The thing is,' she went on slowly, 'we've been able to raise quite a lot of money for the rescue centre, and I'm really pleased. And I know you've been able to raise quite a lot for Hatherington House, too. But ... well, Josie and I, we sort of know your grandad a bit. Not like you do, obviously, but ...'

Sometimes Sarah can never get her words out, can she, **God!**

'But, if it's all right with you, Kevin,' she managed at last, 'we'd like to give half the money we've raised to Hatherington House, too. That way, we'll be helping the animals at the rescue centre **and** *people like your grandad. And that's what we want to do, so ... I hope it's OK.'*

Kevin's mouth was wide open! He was staring. I'm not sure he could quite take in what Sarah was saying. I'm still not sure I can take it in either! But he nodded. He didn't speak, not straightaway, he just nodded. Then we went into the park together, God, and Kevin told us all about his grandad. He talked to us for ages.

When he left to go home, Kevin said, 'The pantomime was a good idea. You Topz deserved to be first.'

You see? When I said incredible, **I meant INCREDIBLE!**

But we don't deserve to be first nearly as much as You do, God. And I'm going to try to remember it every single day! Because when **You're** *first – well – that's when miracles can happen.*

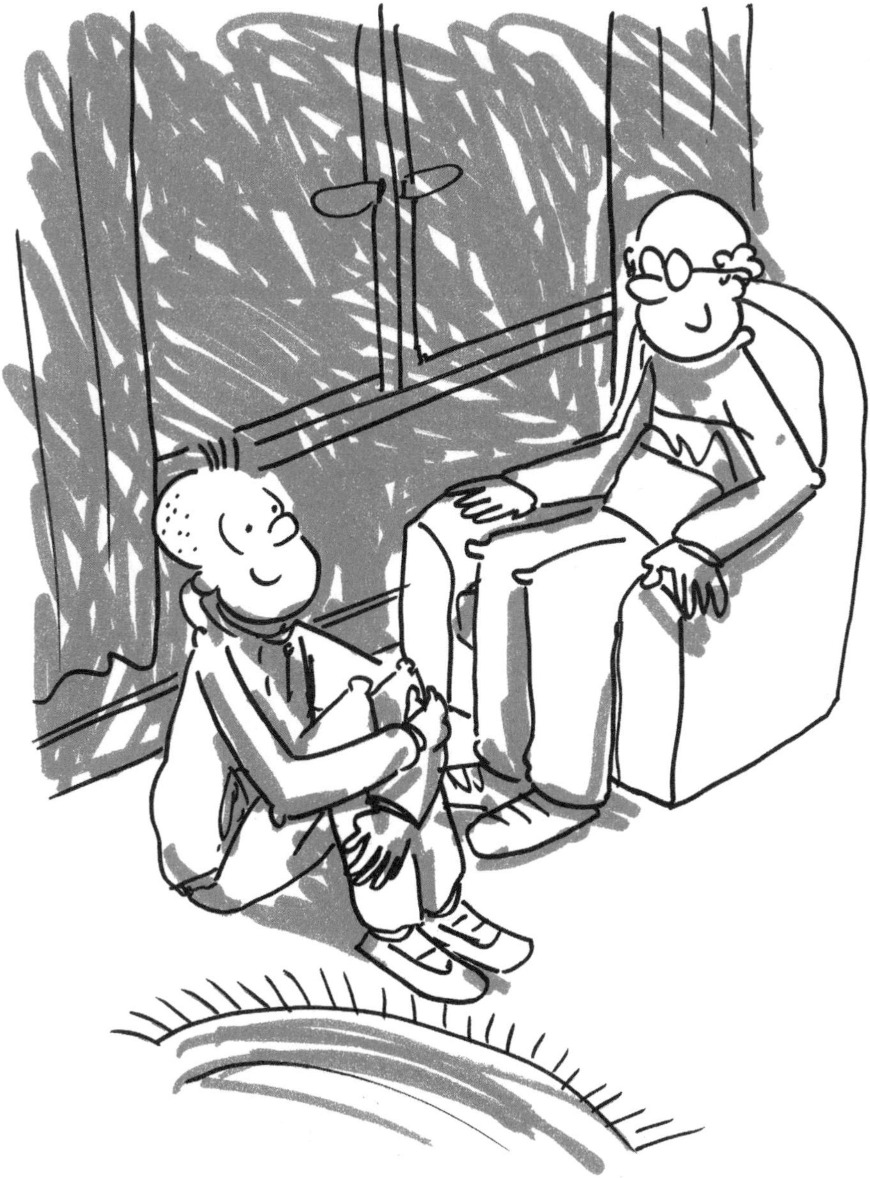

More SECRET STORIES!

Why not try the others in the series?

Dixons Den
New to Holly Hill, Saf befriends Kevin 'the Dixon', who shows her the secret Dixons' den. Furious with Saf, the other Dixons make trouble. Can Saf trust anyone anymore? Can she trust God?
ISBN: 978-1-85345-690-9

Dixons and the Wolf
Rick the Dixon convinces Sarah from the Topz Gang to keep a secret. Rick needs help to look after Wolf the dog. Sarah agrees but she's worried. Is Rick telling the truth about Wolf?
ISBN: 978-1-85345-691-6

One Too Many For Benny
Benny from Topz is fed up with the Dixons Gang, especially Clyde who always seems to be looking for trouble. But maybe things are not quite as they seem ...
ISBN: 978-1-85345-915-3

For current prices, visit **www.cwr.org.uk/store**
Available online or from Christian bookshops.

Boys Only and Just for Girls

These special editions of *Topz Secret Diaries* will help you discover things about yourself and God with questions and quizzes, engaging puzzles, word searches, doodles, lists to write and more.

Topz Secret Diaries: Boys Only
ISBN: 978-1-85345-596-4
126-page paperbacks, 129x197mm

Topz Secret Diaries: Just for Girls
ISBN: 978-1-85345-597-1
126-page paperbacks, 129x197mm

Benny's Barmy Bits
ISBN: 978-1-85345-431-8

Danny's Daring Days
ISBN: 978-1-85345-502-5

Dave's Dizzy Doodles
ISBN: 978-1-85345-552-0

Gruff & Saucy's Topzy-Turvy Tales
ISBN: 978-1-85345-553-7

John's Jam-Packed Jottings
ISBN: 978-1-85345-503-2

Josie's Jazzy Journal
ISBN: 978-1-85345-457-8

Paul's Potty Pages
ISBN: 978-1-85345-456-1

Sarah's Secret Scribblings
ISBN: 978-1-85345-432-5

Go to **www.cwr.org.uk/store**, call 01252 784700 or visit a Christian bookshop.

Topz is a colourful daily devotional for 7- to 11-year-olds.

In each issue the Topz Gang teach children biblical truths through word games, puzzles, riddles, cartoons, competitions, simple prayers and daily Bible readings.

Available as an annual subscription **£15.95** (6 bimonthly issues includes p&p) or as single issues **£2.95**.

Go to **www.cwr.org.uk/store**, call 01252 784700 or visit a Christian bookshop.

Prices correct at time of printing.